Published by On the W

Cover Design by Holly Henry

For Rafe and Maren

1

Maddie Larkin hated the snow. She didn't trust it.

Snow had stolen her father.

Ten years ago, when Maddie was a newborn, her dad had gone out in a blizzard to buy some nappies and never came back. He'd even left his phone behind, and a steaming mug of coffee, while he nipped to the Co-op.

When the police began their search for him no one at the Co-op could recall seeing him at all. He'd simply vanished. But Maddie knew what had happened; he'd been snatched by the snow.

Luckily, the valley that her hometown of Wistwell nestled in rarely saw the fluffy white stuff; it was a warm pocket snuggled between gently rolling hills.

But this year was different. December arrived in a howl of icy winds that spat chips of frozen ice into stinging eyes. By the sixteenth, real snow blew in – born by a sub-zero blast all the way from Siberia – and settled in for the festive season.

The kids at school were delirious with excitement. Maddie's friends begged her to lie down and make snow angels. They built snowmen and tossed snowballs – especially the boys, who threw them hard enough to really hurt – but Maddie wanted none of it.

Sometimes Maddie missed having a dad. Some of the kids at school seemed to get a new one every couple of years. Most had just one living at home with their mum, while others had a dad tucked away elsewhere who they got to see at weekends and on birthdays. Daniel Hargate, in year six, had two dads but no mum.

On the last day of term Maddie trudged home in her wellies, insulated against the evil snow by coat, scarf, stripey hat, and mittens. Only her eyes peeped out, flakes settling on her lashes. Officially term shouldn't end until next Wednesday but as the forecast was for more snow and a deep freeze, the authorities had decided it was best to finish early and shut the school at lunchtime. Most of the kids, including her best friends, Suzy and Daisy, were going sledding on Topton Hill, but they knew better than to try and make her play in the snow.

Maddie lived in a flat over her mother's florist shop, two doors down from Mr Steiner's German Bakery. The bakery was famous for miles around. It brought visitors to the village, particularly in the run up to Christmas when German baked goods were in great demand. Mr Steiner baked *kokosmakronen, lebkuchen* and *spekulatius* if you were fond of cookies and biscuits, but what he was really known for was his fabulous *kuchen* and *torte* – cakes – and at Christmas time his *marzipanstollen* reigned supreme.

Maddie didn't go to the bakery as much since Mrs Steiner had died last December. She missed Mrs Steiner a lot. She'd had soft silver hair and pretty brown eyes that smiled when Maddie came in clutching her money.

She'd often slipped Maddie an extra pretzel or a spritz cookie (*spritzgebäck,* Mr Steiner called them).

Maddie's mother loved stollen. The first slice of seasonal stollen was a cause for celebration in their household, even though Maddie didn't actually like marzipan. She had *lebkuchen* (gingerbread) instead, with hot chocolate served in her special Christmas mug, while her mum and Maddie's grandma, Nanny Dot, ate their stollen off dainty china plates.

Last night had been the real start of Christmas for them.

"I dedicate this slice of stollen to the memory of Betty Steiner," Nanny Dot said, just before she took her first bite.

They raised their plates and clinked them, two stollen slices, and a gingerbread cookie, in tribute to Mrs Steiner.

"I'm glad Mr Steiner decided to keep the bakery open," Maddie's mum said. "For a while it looked like he wouldn't reopen, poor man."

"Best thing for him is to keep busy," Nanny Dot replied. "Like I did when your dad passed."

Maddie had never known Granddad Fred. He had died when her mother was just a little girl. Men didn't seem to fare so well in their family.

Mum swallowed her stollen. She sighed with pleasure. "Delicious," she declared. "Perhaps his best ever. Slightly salty but in a way that sets off the marzipan wonderfully. How's your gingerbread, Maddie?"

"Yummy," Maddie said. "Just the right amount of chewy."

They munched happily for a few minutes.

"When are we going to put the tree up?" Maddie asked.

"Saturday night," Mum said.

"Yay!" Maddie sang. "The tree, the tree." She loved Christmas.

Yet the next day – the last day of term – Maddie woke feeling unusually glum. It had stopped snowing but the pavements were caked with a crust of treacherous snow-compacted ice. She put her gloominess down to this.

Her mum was no better. Maddie found her slumped at the kitchen table, tucking into another slice of stollen. She started guiltily as Maddie walked in.

"Not a very sensible breakfast, I know," she said. "But I need something sweet to pick me up this morning." She'd taken a swig of strong coffee. "Do you want toast or cereal?"

"Not bothered," Maddie said, flopping into a chair.

"I hope we're not coming down with something," her mum sighed. "I feel exhausted."

Later, as she trudged home from school, Maddie saw a long queue trailing out of the bakery, and remembered that she was supposed to pick up a *sachertorte* cake for her mother. She'd been given the money.

Maddie took her place at the end of the line, stamping her feet to keep her toes warm. The line shuffled forwards as slowly as the clock in a maths lesson. A couple of people gave up, huffing their disgust at the slow service.

As Maddie drew level with the window she could see Mr Steiner behind the counter, looking hot and flustered as he struggled to manage on his own.

It was Mrs Steiner, Maddie remembered, who had cheerfully and efficiently put together the orders while Mr Steiner ran the cash register or brought out the baked goods. “Three chocolate Santas, a marzipanstollen and a butterstollen, two dozen poppy seed rolls and a rye loaf. There you go. Apple strudel? Of course. Ah, Mrs Smith, your Linzer torte is ready. Try a Christmas cookie. They’re free.”

Mrs Steiner had been unflusterable. Peering through the glass, Maddie felt her absence anew. Poor Mr Steiner looked lost without her.

Without thinking Maddie ran past the line of customers, squeezing past the ones blocking the door, and into the shop.

“Hey, little girl,” a man grumbled. “Can’t you see the queue?”

Maddie ignored him, pushing to the front, where she didn’t even stop, ducking under the flap of the wooden counter to pop up next to Mr Steiner

He blinked at her with his blue eyes. His face was red. “Maddie?”

"Don't worry, Mr Steiner," Maddie said, flinging her coat into the passage that led to the kitchen. "I'll help you."

"I don't think that is legal," Mr Steiner said in his soft German accent. "You are too young."

"Let her help," a woman waiting to be served said. "You look like you need it."

"I know where everything is," Maddie said. "I used to watch Mrs Steiner all the time."

At the mention of his wife's name, Mr Steiner flinched, but his expression softened. "So you did," he nodded. Turning to the woman, he asked "What is your order?"

"Two marzipanstollen and a butterstollen," she answered, reading off her list. "And a loaf of pumpernickel."

Maddie knew exactly where to find each item and packed them into bags – the paper ones with Steiner's German Bakery stamped on the front – while Mr Steiner rang up the order and gave the woman her change.

They worked this system efficiently until the bakery was almost empty of goods and customers.

"I can't believe you know where everything is exactly," Mr Steiner declared. "Only my wife knew that."

"I used to help her re-stock the shop sometimes," Maddie said. "On Monday afternoons after school."

Mr Steiner looked surprised. "Did you?"

"Uhuh," Maddie nodded. "You were with your jumper friends."

Now Mr Steiner looked bewildered. "My jumper friends?"

"Yes, Mrs Steiner said on Mondays you practised with your jumper band."

"Oh!" Mr Steiner smiled. "My Oompah band."

Maddie was about to ask what an Oompah band was when Nanny Dot burst into the shop.

"There you are," she snapped. "I thought you'd been abducted. You had me worried sick."

Maddie knew that adults always got angry when they said they were worried about you. Why was that?

"Sorry, Nanny. I was just helping Mr Steiner. It was *really* busy in here."

"It's very busy in our shop too," Nanny said, glaring at Mr Steiner.

"But Mr Steiner was on his own," Maddie protested.

"You should have hired someone to help you," Nanny Dot told Mr Steiner. "I don't know about Germany but in England we don't use child labour."

"Nanny!" Maddie gasped. She had never heard Nanny say something so mean or unfair. In fact Nanny Dot was usually the nicest person she knew.

Mr Steiner stiffened. "Madeleine is a very kind little girl, Mrs Flowers. But you are quite right." He turned to Maddie, his face softening. "Thank you so much, Maddie, for your help. My wife would have been very proud of you today. Now, there isn't much left but you must take whatever there is in payment." He indicated to the mostly empty shelves.

"Oh no!" Maddie remembered her original task. "I was supposed to pick up a *sachertorte* for mum." She glanced sheepishly at Nanny Dot. "I forgot and now we've sold them all." She chewed her lower lip.

"Wait," Mr Steiner said. He disappeared into the bakery kitchen and came back bearing the most beautiful, chocolate satin *Sachertorte*. It was easily the largest cake Maddie had ever seen.

It looked very expensive. Nanny Dot gulped, pulling out her purse.

"I made it for a customer's party," Mr Steiner explained. "But I can make another. You must take it."

"How much?" Nanny Dot asked.

Mr Steiner gave her a contemptuous look. "There is no charge, Mrs Flowers. It is payment – and not enough at that – for Maddie's help."

"Oh, Mr Steiner," Maddie breathed. "I can't."

"You can and you will," Mr Steiner said. "I will put it in a box, *ja*? And you will tell all your friends to come and eat your cake." He added the last bag of unsold butter cookies and three pretzels. "There," he said. "Now I can close for the day; there is nothing left to sell."

Nanny Dot took the cookies and pretzels wordlessly as Maddie wrapped her arms around the enormous cake box and carried it out like treasure.

At the door Nanny Dot paused. "I'm sorry about what I said," she said unhappily. "I don't know what's wrong with me today. I'm so out of sorts."

Mr Steiner, who had come to lock the door and turn the closed sign after them, nodded. "I understand. It is the time of year, *nein*? It is very stressful."

"I suppose so," Nanny Dot agreed. "But usually I love it. Oh," she said, reaching out to touch his hand. "It must be very hard for you … it was this time last year..."

She meant it was this time last year that Mrs Steiner had died but couldn't finish the sentence.

"*Ja*," Mr Steiner said, looking away.

"I'm so sorry."

"*Ja*," he said again and gently closed the door.

2

Nanny usually ran the flower shop on Saturdays so that Mum could do the shopping and spend some time with Maddie, but the last Saturday before Christmas was always particularly busy so Maddie helped Nanny Dot make up the Christmas wreaths in the back of the shop while Mum and her seventeen-year-old shop-assistant, Sally Holson, served the customers. At this time of year their Christmas wreaths and holly sprigs sold as fast as Mr Steiner's stollen cakes, and she and Nanny would be hard-pressed to keep up with demand. It was a tradition she loved.

Usually.

Once again she'd woken up feeling miserable. It must be the snow, she thought. I wish it would all blow away.

Mum was grumpy too. "I shouldn't have eaten all those butter cookies," she grumbled. "I feel like a fat slug and just as slow."

Last night Maddie, Mum and Nanny had finished the cookies in front of the TV. They were as delicious as always but the more they ate the worse they seemed to feel. Luckily, Mum had forbidden them to touch the *sachertorte*. She was going to cut the cake into small portions to serve her customers as a special Christmas treat.

The shop was bustling. Usually no one was more delighted by the continual 'ka-ching' of the cash register than Nanny Dot, but she had arrived in a bad mood. As the morning went on her wreaths began looking a bit bedraggled and sparse as though she couldn't be bothered. Maddie tried to brighten them up with berries and ribbons but her spirits were flagging too.

Mum sent a few of the wreaths back via Sally, with the message that they weren't good enough and to put a little effort in.

Sally, embarrassed to be the message bearer was mortified when Nanny Dot burst into angry tears, stamping into the shop to confront her daughter.

Maddie shared Sally's feelings.

Soon Mum was in tears too as she and Nanny bickered. A few customers scurried away while others stayed to enjoy the scene.

One of Daniel Hargate's dads – Maddie was never sure which was which as they were both very handsome – calmed the situation down. Soon everyone was laughing about the things Christmas did to perfectly rational people, all the stress and anxiety and unrealistic expectations sent them a little loopy.

Maddie had heard of this sort of thing before. One year, Suzy's normally lovely mum threw the under-cooked turkey out of the kitchen window while all of Suzy's relatives sat at the dinner table waiting for dinner.

"Why do grownups go crazy at Christmas?" Suzy had asked. "Christmas is wonderful."

Mum and Nanny hugged, wiped away their tears, and by early afternoon everyone, Maddie included, was feeling better.

"There's plenty of cake left," Mum said to Maddie. "Why don't you call Suzy and Daisy to come over and have some?"

Suzy and Daisy arrived later, bursting with the news that Jake Burns had broken his arm when he'd lost control of his sled and smashed into a tree.

Jake was the best looking boy in their class so Maddie knew he'd get a lot of signatures on his cast. If she didn't feel too shy maybe she'd even add one herself. That opportunity aside, Jake's accident just went to show why snow couldn't be trusted.

They wolfed the cake in the back room of the shop, nattering and giggling, washing it down with orange squash. Suzy declared it tasted like a chocolate orange.

The florist's shop shut at four on Saturdays. Mum said anyone who hadn't sorted out their flower needs by that stage in the weekend was a dead loss or didn't care for blooms. She cashed up as Sally and Nanny Dot brought the pavement displays inside.

"What are you getting for Christmas?" Daisy asked Maddie.

"I dunno," Maddie said. "I'm hoping for a new bike. Mine's so old. It's too small for me now. I'd love a red one, with a basket on front."

As she said this, Maddie was suddenly struck by a wave of sadness. She pictured her old bike, lying neglected in the shed in their back garden and felt a lump rise in her throat. Poor bike.

"The best present I ever had was my Belle doll," Daisy sighed. "I loved her."

"I still hate your brother for throwing her in the river," Suzy said.

"Won't your mum get you another one?" Maddie asked.

"It won't be the same." Daisy's lower lip trembled. "She won't be *my* Belle."

All three girls stood in morose silence.

"I miss my granddad," Suzy whispered.

"I miss Mrs Steiner," Maddie said. "And my Dad."

Daisy started to cry first, setting off the other two.

"I feel so sad," Maddie moaned. They clutched each other's hands, huddling together in a little weepy circle.

"Whatever's going on?" Mum's voice broke through.

The girls looked up to see Mum and Suzy's mum, Mrs Bailey, standing in the doorway staring at them with alarm.

"We just feel so sad," Suzy said, running to wrap her arms around her mother's waist.

"Have you girls been arguing?" Mrs Bailey asked.

All three shook their heads vigorously.

Mum frowned. "It's been a funny day. Lots of people seem out of sorts. Sad or tetchy. I've felt the same way."

"Maybe it's the weather," Mrs Bailey said. "And it gets dark so early." She gave Suzy a squeeze. "C'mon silly. Time to go. Daisy, your mum asked me to drop you off."

"Take a slice of torte with you," Mum offered. "I've been saving mine to have with a cup of tea at home."

"If you're sure," Mrs Bailey said. "Is it from Steiner's?" Her eyes lit up at Mum's nod.

They didn't decorate the tree that night after all. At seven o' clock mum declared she had a cracking headache and took herself to bed, while Nanny Dot sniffled her way through a showing of It's a Wonderful Life on Film Four, outright bawling towards the end.

Maddie hated the film and locked herself in her room. She tried painting a Christmas card for Mum but the colours came out blotchy and muddy looking.

"Oh, this is going to be the worst Christmas ever," she cried, tearing it up.

Outside it began to snow again.

#

Fortunately everyone was cheerier on Sunday morning. Nanny Dot sung carols as she folded the sofa bed away. Nanny Dot didn't actually live with them – she had her own small house half a mile away – but she often stayed overnight on the sofa bed, especially on Saturdays.

The sky was a brilliant blue and the sun made the snow sparkle. Even Maddie had to admit it looked pretty.

"It's like a Christmas card," Nanny said. "Not many sleeps now."

"Six," Maddie said, searching for the 19th on her advent calendar. She popped the chocolate in her mouth. Tomorrow it would be Mum's turn.

"Morning," Mum said appearing in the kitchen. She looked perkier than she had last night.

"Can we do the tree this morning?" Maddie said.

Mum poured herself a cup of tea from the pot which was wrapped in a Christmas pudding cosy. "Don't you want to wait until it's dark?"

"I can't wait any longer," Maddie begged. "Pleeeeeeeeeeeze."

Mum laughed. "Okay. I'll just have some toast. You and Nanny start putting up the tree."

"Yay!" Maddie yelled.

She and Nanny pulled the composite parts of the artificial tree out of a box barely held together with years of parcel tape.

Some of the kids at school claimed artificial trees were rubbish and only real ones were good enough.

Maddie didn't agree. They didn't know the pleasure of getting the same tree out year after year, like seeing an old friend you didn't even know you were missing until they visited again. Plus Maddie liked trees; she didn't want to think of them being chopped down. It seemed a mean thing to do, although Mum insisted it didn't hurt them.

"Put on some music, Maddie," Nanny called. She was checking the lights before they went on the tree. There was nothing worse, Nanny said, than finding the lights didn't work after you'd fought to wrap them around the tree.

Maddie chose her favourite soundtrack: A Muppet Christmas Carol. Magic began to fill the air.

"Good choice," Mum said, coming into the lounge with her toast and tea to take a directorial seat on the sofa.

The morning was a happy one. They hung years' worth of collected and homemade decorations on the tree, exclaiming over each one, welcoming it back to the light after months of lying in a dark box in the loft. Then they made brightly patterned paper chains, festooning them around the flat, adding hanging baubles and bells to the inverted Vs between the swags.

Mum hung one of their handmade wreaths on the inside of the flat's front door and arranged a vase of holly and ivy on the mantelpiece.

It all looked so jolly.

Then they sat down to admire the handiwork and celebrate with a piece of stollen and coffee for Mum and Nanny while Maddie had a large glass of fizzy Coca Cola - something she was only allowed occasionally.

The sunshine had disappeared behind thick clouds that threatened more snow. No one minded because the gloom made the tree lights glow more vibrantly. They gazed at it in peaceful wonder.

"Oh," Mum said. "I forgot. Maddie I bought you your own little tree and lights for your room."

"Really?" Maddie bounced up, delighted. "Where is it?"

"I'll get it." Mum went into her bedroom – a place Maddie was banned from in the run up to Christmas although it was no longer necessary since three years ago Maddie had broken the rules and sneaked in to find her presents in the bottom of Mum's wardrobe. It had completely ruined the surprise on Christmas day and Maddie had been so ashamed she'd never told Mum or Nanny what she'd done.

Mum returned with a bag from Wilkos. In it was a tabletop-size tree, a string of white lights and a carton of pretty baubles in pink, silver, and gold. There was a glittery silver star for the top.

"Thank you!" Maddie breathed. "I'm going to put it up right now."

It took her half an hour to set up the tree on top of her desk. It twinkled gorgeously.

Maddie went to fetch Mum and Nanny. They'd cleared away their plates and taken them to the kitchen. Maddie heard Mum's voice, followed by Nanny's muted reply. She was about to push open the door when she realised Mum's voice sounded wrong. It cracked the way Maddie's did when she was trying not to cry.

Maddie held her breath and listened.

"It must be the snow," Mum said. "I haven't thought about him for so long – haven't let myself – but for the last couple of days it's all I've thought about. How he could have left us; whether he's alive or dead. I feel like it's only just happened."

Maddie gasped. Mum was taking about Dad. She never did that.

"I know," Nanny soothed. "I know. I've been thinking about him too."

Maddie shook her head, bewildered. What was happening? Why was everyone so sad this year?

Maddie tiptoed back to her room, shutting the door quietly. A few minutes later someone knocked on her bedroom door.

"Yeah?"

Mum peered into the room. She smiled weakly when she saw the little tree. "Very pretty," she said, crossing to the bed to give Maddie a kiss. "Just like my favourite daughter."

It seemed to Maddie that Mum's hug was tighter than usual. Maddie leaned into her.

"I need to go the supermarket," Mum said, finally releasing her. "Do you want to come or stay here with Nanny?"

"I'll come," Maddie said, hopping off the bed.

Nanny was sitting at the kitchen table with a glass of sherry and a grim expression. Before her she had a pile of Christmas cards to write.

"Waste of paper," she muttered.

"Nanny!" Maddie reminded her. "You love cards."

"I know," Nanny sighed. "I'm just being a humbug. Here," she handed Maddie a card. "Drop this off at Mr Steiner's would you?"

Maddie took the card.

Outside Mum said. "I'll de-ice the car and get it warmed up while you drop the card round."

The gritter had cleared the road but today the pavements were snowy as none of the shopkeepers had salted their fronts. Maddie clomped carefully through the snow to the bakery. On a Sunday – even before Christmas – it was shuttered and locked up tight. It was the same on Mondays.

But Maddie could see the lights were on in the back kitchen where Mr Steiner did his baking, so she set off down the narrow alleyway between the bakery and the neighbouring post-office to the back door. It was the way she used to take on Monday afternoons when she helped out Mrs Steiner.

Maddie saw Mr Steiner through the window. He was kneading dough on a large table, hands and forearms covered in flour. She was about to knock when she noticed a fat teardrop splash onto the dough. It was followed by another and another. More and more tears melted into the mixture, yet Mr Steiner kept on kneading, as though he didn't even know he was crying.

The strains of Stille Nacht wafted through the glass. Maddie knew it as the German version of Silent Night.

She turned away.

Was every person in town sad?

Her heart was heavy as she crept back up the entry and round to the front of the bakery. She slid the card into the letter slot on the front door and scurried over to the car belching fumes into the afternoon air.

Her mum waited behind the wheel.

"Did you give it to him?" Mum asked, as Maddie belted herself in. Maddie shook her head and told Mum what she'd seen.

"Oh, that poor man," Mum said. "It was about this time last year he lost his wife. I wonder what he's doing for Christmas. I hope he's got somewhere to go."

Maddie considered it. "Maybe we could invite him?"

Mum 'ummed' non-committally. "Well, we'll see what Nanny Dot thinks. I'm sure he's already had plenty of invitations."

3

Maddie shot up in bed. Her bedside clock read twelve-thirty and the flat was quiet. Nanny had gone home and Mum was asleep. For a moment Maddie didn't know why she'd woken so suddenly then the realisation hit her again. Her dreaming brain had worked out the cause of everyone's misery.

It was Mr Steiner's baking.

Mum, Nanny Dot, herself, Daisy and Suzy: all of them felt weepy after eating Mr Steiner's delicious goodies. Why? Normally cookies and cakes made Maddie happy; the perfect sugar and fat combo, her Mum liked to say.

Mr Steiner's baking had the regular stuff: sugar, eggs, butter, flour, spices, fruit and nuts, yeast for the breads, along with all the other ingredients that normally went into the mixes.

This year it also had tears. Mr Steiner grieved when he baked. He missed Mrs Steiner and his sadness went into the baking.

Poor Mr Steiner, Maddie thought. Poor, poor Mr Steiner. But her sympathy was also tempered by practicality.

Mr Steiner was going to ruin Christmas for a lot of people. Nearly everyone in town bought something from Steiner's for festive feasting. He was going to make them miserable.

Maddie chewed at her thumbnail. What could she do? She knew Mum wouldn't believe her. She didn't put up with any 'of that kind of nonsense'. She'd never believed that Father Christmas was real. She'd definitely pooh-pooh the idea that Mr Steiner's tears were affecting his baking, although after Maddie had told her she'd seen Mr Steiner crying into his dough, Mum said it put her off the stollen. "Not very hygienic," she said.

At least that was a good thing, Maddie thought, if it meant Mum stopped eating the stollen. Still, to be on the safe side, Maddie crept out of her bedroom to the kitchen and removed the last bit of stollen from the snowman tin and put it in a sandwich bag.

"Maddie?" her mother's sleepy voice called from her bedroom.

Maddie froze. Mum was such a light sleeper. "Just going to the toilet, mum," she called back. "I'm okay."

She tiptoed into the bathroom, waited a moment before flushing the loo, and returned to bed.

Back under the covers, knees drawn up to her chest, Maddie examined the piece of stollen. It looked so innocent. What she needed was to test her theory, just like Mr Stevens said they should do in science class.

She could try the stollen on herself but she hated the taste of marzipan so much that even in the name of science she couldn't bring herself to eat it.

She needed a human guinea pig; someone who was nearly always happy.

Lucy Henry was probably the most cheerful person Maddie had ever met. She was in Maddie's class and while she wasn't one of her best friends, Maddie went to her birthday parties every year and occasionally went round to play at her house. To be honest, Maddie found Lucy's bouncy good cheer a bit weird at times.

Should she visit Lucy in the morning and offer her the stollen? Her conscience answered: No. It wasn't fair to make Lucy feel unhappy.

Who would it be fair to try it on?

After a moment, Maddie smiled rather wickedly.

She had the perfect plan.

#

George Wilkins was tall for his age, strong and stocky, with a mean kind of cunning. He was the school bully and ruled the swings area in the park. He often found ways to annoy Maddie – pulling down her hood, tying her shoes laces together, tapping her on the shoulder in class to show off a disgusting snot bubble – but he didn't beat her up the way he did some of the younger boys.

Maddie despised him. Nanny Dot said George probably fancied Maddie, or he would leave her alone. He was trying to impress her. Maddie thought Nanny Dot was mad. The idea that George Wilkins might like her was too repulsive to consider.

Bracing herself, Maddie walked past the swings. There were a lot of kids in the park today. With school broken up and Christmas only days away, spirits were high. Maddie cringed every time a snowball came whizzing past her but carried on. She had a mission.

George was in his usual place, hogging the swings with his stupid friends. As soon as he saw Maddie he scooped up a snowball and hurled it her way. It exploded against her well-padded anorak, making her squeal. Tilting her head up, she carried on until she reached a bench nearby. The seat was icy but she forced herself to sit on it and take off her gloves. Carefully, as though it was precious, Maddie took the stollen out of her pocket and unwrapped it. She pretended she was going to take a bite when George appeared in front of her and snatched it away.

He laughed, holding it out of reach. “Cool. Thanks for the present, Maddie.”

“It’s not for you,” Maddie said, thrusting to her feet. “You give it back.”

George stuffed the whole piece in his wide mouth. “Gi wa ba?” he spluttered, spraying her with soggy crumbs. He turned to his friends who were laughing.

"You're a pig," Maddie said, pushing past him. "I hope you choke."

Four more snowballs hit her as she stomped away, curtesy of George and his pals but Maddie kept going.

Out of the park gates and around the corner she hugged herself tightly. It had worked! Stupid George had done exactly what she thought he would. Quickly, Maddie retrieved a large carrier bag she'd hidden behind a bin. In it was her parka with the hood that zipped up like a snout so that her face was almost completely hidden. It was tight as she'd grown this year but Mum hadn't got round to getting rid of the charity bags yet, so with some rooting around, Maddie had found it this morning. She could just about squeeze into it and zip up the hood.

Whipping off her cerise anorak, Maddie stuffed it into the bag and changed into the parka.

This time she took the carrier with her and ambled back into the park, desperately hoping she wouldn't be recognised by George and his mates. Taking a different path, one that circled the perimeter, she slowly walked around it, keeping an eye on George's little gang, right across the park. On the playing field kids and adults were building snowmen and chasing each other in the snow. A few dogs ran around, barking excitedly.

Three quarters of the way round Maddie positioned herself behind a sycamore tree to keep a watch on the swing area.

George monkeyed around with his friends, hanging off the swings, stuffing snow down each others' backs and scaring off the smaller kids. When a man with a little boy came to use the swings they moved back a few paces, hanging out until the pair left.

Maddie watched for half an hour, stamping her feet to keep warm, glad of the snug parka hood.

She was beginning to think her experiment had failed when a Golden Labrador ran up to the boys, chasing a ball.

George scooped up the ball before the labrador reached it and held it up, much as he had the stollen piece. The dog barked and wagged its tail, skipping from side to side, waiting for George to throw the ball.

George feinted from left to right, teasing the dog.

Maddie frowned, thinking George would do something mean, like throw the ball over the park wall where the dog couldn't follow. Instead, George threw it in a straight line onto the grass, sending the lab whirling after it.

George laughed as he watched it run to catch the ball, his expression caught in a rare instance of open joy.

Maddie stared at him. She saw the moment his face crumpled, mouth sliding downwards into an unhappy arch, eyes scrunching up as he sank to his knees.

A moment later George Wilkins was bawling like a toddler who's fallen over and scraped his knee.

His friends gaped at him, astounded. This was not the George they knew, this crybaby blubbing in the snow. For a few moments no one moved until Mark Sands tentatively approached him.

Maddie left her hiding place and hurried along the path so she could catch what they said. She slowed a little as she drew parallel. Mark asked George what was wrong.

"I miss Scarface," George wailed. "I m…m…miss my dog."

Maddie felt sorry for him. Years ago she'd seen George Wilkins walking a squat dog. It had been hit by a car and George had taken a whole week off school after it happened. Their year three teacher, Miss Popple, told them to be kind to George when he returned.

The Monday he came back, Suzy had asked him if he was all right. He'd punched her in the stomach.

Remembering that part, Maddie felt better.

She scurried away, leaving George behind to wallow in his misery. Her stomach fizzed with excitement. Her theory was correct. Mr Steiner's stollen had even made the toughest boy in school break down and cry. His baking really was magic.

Now, what could she do about it?

As Mum and Sally were managing the shop perfectly well between them, Nanny suggested she and Maddie go to the library. Maddie agreed as she had a stack of books to return and wanted to see if they'd got in the new Dixie McKenna mystery. Dixie was her favourite heroine.

The latest Dixie was out on loan, much to Maddie's disappointment, so she chose the Mystery of the Revolving Mirror, although she'd read it a zillion times before.

"I'll never get to read the new one," Maddie grumbled.

"Wait to see what Santa brings you," Nanny Dot said. "You never know."

"Santa's not real, Nanny," Maddie said. "Mum says."

Nanny tutted. "Sometimes your mother is as much fun as a slap in the face with a wet fish."

Maddie giggled. "You can't say that!"

"I just did," Nanny said. "But don't tell her." She flashed Maddie a conspiratorial grin.

It was good to see Nanny back to normal.

"Nanny," Maddie said, lowering her voice. "If I tell you something will you promise to believe me?"

Nanny peered at her. "Tell me over a hot chocolate, and I promise to believe you."

When they were snug in a corner table at the Blue Teapot and the waitress had delivered hot chocolates topped with whipped cream and marshmallows, Nanny asked: "So what is it you want to tell me?"

Maddie took a deep breath. Suddenly she didn't want to say it. "You're going to think I'm silly."

"Try me," Nanny Dot winked.

"Well," Maddie said. "It's Mr Steiner's cakes. I think they make people feel sad."

"Why?" Nanny asked this perfectly seriously, not a hint of teasing in her voice.

Maddie told Nanny her theory and described the stollen experiment. The words tumbled out of her. "Then George started crying about his dead dog and I knew it was the stollen that caused it. You know, George Wilkins, Nanny. He's a horrid boy."

Nanny nodded. "Yes," she said. "His father's the same. The apple doesn't fall far from the tree."

"So you believe me, Nanny?"

"I think it's a very good theory," Nanny said. "But we need to test it out some more."

"How?"

"Well, it seems to me," Nanny said, leaning forward. "If you're right and Mr Steiner's sadness is magically infecting his baking then it might work the opposite way too."

"What do you mean?" Maddie asked, wide-eyed.

"I mean if we can make Mr Steiner happy when he bakes maybe his baking will make those who eat it happy too."

"Yes!" Maddie breathed. "That's clever, Nanny Dot."

"Thank you," Nanny Dot preened.

"But how can we make him happy and then try out his baking on someone miserable?"

"Ah, now. We'll have to figure that one out. We'd better drink our hot chocolates before they go cold."

They set to, spooning in marshmallows and whipped cream, before slurping the sweet, warm liquid. Maddie laughed at Nanny's cream moustache and laughed even harder when Nanny flipped open a compact mirror and showed Maddie her own chocolate smile and whipped cream whiskers.

"Dorothy Flowers," a man's voice interrupted their mirth. "How charming to see you."

Nanny Dot looked up to see a man with greying hair smiling down at her. Quickly, she grabbed a napkin and wiped the cream off her face, turning a delicate shade of pink.

Maddie watched, intrigued. She had never, ever seen Nanny Dot look embarrassed.

"Hello Phil," Nanny said, recovering herself. "Long time, no see."

"Indeed," Phil beamed down at her. "You haven't changed a bit. And who's this lovely lady?" He nodded to Maddie.

"This is my granddaughter, Madeleine," Nanny Dot introduced her. "Maddie, this is Mr Turner."

"Enchanted," Mr Turner said, but his eyes were already back on Nanny. "Do you still play?"

"Oh no," Nanny Dot laughed. Her hand fluttered to her hair. "I haven't picked up my trumpet for years."

"Pity," Mr Turner said. "You were so good."

"You play the trumpet?" Maddie gasped.

"I used to," Nanny said. "A long time ago." She deflected the attention back to Mr Turner. "What about you? Are you still playing?"

"In an Oompah band of all things," Mr Turner said. "More for fun than anything, although we do a few concerts and benefits. We're doing one at a homeless hostel in Great Alderton on Christmas Eve – just in the afternoon."

"An Oompah band?" Maddie asked. "Do you know Mr Steiner?"

For the first time Mr Turner focussed on her properly. He looked surprised. "Hans Steiner? Indeed I do. He was our accordion player but I'm afraid he stopped playing after his wife died. A great shame as we haven't found anyone to really replace him. In fact, I've got a card for him. I was going to drop it off."

"Maddie can give it to him," Nanny said. "She lives two doors from the bakery."

"Very kind of you," Mr Turner said, searching inside his jacket until he found the card.

Maddie noticed he had hair growing out of his nostrils. It put her off her hot chocolate so she looked away.

"Wistwell seems to be doing well," Mr Turner said. "Since Marjorie went I've been thinking of moving back to Wistwell."

"Oh, I'm sorry," Nanny said. "I hadn't heard she'd passed away."

Mr Turner snorted. "She didn't. She left me for a tuba player six months ago."

"Oh dear," Nanny Dot said in a slightly strangled voice. "How awful for you." It was the voice she used when she was trying not to laugh. She hid her mouth behind a paper napkin.

"You've still got a naughty streak, Dorothy Flowers," Mr Turner said.

Maddie peered up at him. His eyes twinkled with good humour, so she decided she liked him despite his nose hair. Old people were often a little bit ugly; they couldn't help it.

"Anyway, I'd best be going. I've got band practise this afternoon. Give my regards to Hans if you see him and tell him we miss him. Oh and…" Mr Turner paused. "Perhaps if I do decide to move back you might help me find a place?" His gaze on Nanny Dot was so intense it gave Maddie a funny kind of shiver.

Nanny Dot fluttered her eyelashes and held Mr Turner's gaze in a way that excluded Maddie.

"Perhaps I will," Nanny Dot said.

Mr Turner smiled, nodded, and turned to go. "And pick up that trumpet again," he called over his shoulder.

"My, that was unexpected," Nanny sighed, patting her hair again. "It takes me right back."

Maddie fidgeted impatiently. "But what about Mr Steiner," she asked. "What are we going to do about him?"

#

Mr Steiner was behind with his baking. His heart just wasn't in it. Yesterday he'd burnt a whole batch of cookies and his dough hadn't risen. It was a disaster in the run up to Christmas with demand for his goods so high.

Maddie's grandmother was right. He needed to hire help for the shop but the thought of replacing Betty with someone he didn't know was just too depressing. Besides, he didn't have the energy to look for someone.

Betty had loved this time of year.

"Oh Bettina, *mein liebling*, why did you leave me?" Mr Steiner muttered. "I cannot manage without you."

He sat on a stool beside his high baking bench, trying to make himself start.

Perhaps he should have sold the shop after all? But he and Betty had built the business together and it would have felt like selling off her memory. He hadn't even been able to give away her clothes yet; a year after she had passed they still smelt of her favourite perfume and he frequently buried his nose in them.

Oh dear, the tears were threatening again, he'd better get himself moving.

A knock at the kitchen door surprised him. He glanced up to see Maddie Larkin's pink nose almost pressed to the glass, the bobble on her stripey hat bobbing like a robin on a branch.

He lumbered to his feet and went to the door. "Maddie," he said, opening it. "What a surprise? What can I do for you?"

"I have a card for you, Mr Steiner," Maddie said, clutching an envelope in her mittened hand.

"But I already had one from you yesterday," Mr Steiner said.

"It's not from me," Maddie explained. It's from your friend in the Oompah band, Mr Turner."

"Philip?"

"Yes," Maddie said. "Nanny and me bumped into him this morning. He asked me to give you this." She thrust the card towards him.

"Oh. Thank you," Mr Steiner said, taking it. "This is very kind of you."

Maddie continued to stand on the doorstep, gazing up at him expectantly, although Mr Steiner couldn't guess why. "Um," he said. "Thank you again for your help on Saturday, Maddie."

Maddie shrugged. "You're welcome, Mr Steiner. I could help again if you like, with the baking?"

"Oh no," Mr Steiner said, taking a step back from the door. "That is not necessary."

No sooner had he taken his step back than Maddie seemed to see it as an invitation to come in and skipped over the threshold.

She looked round with interest at all the ingredients laid out on the counters and all the baking equipment stacked up or hanging from hooks on the walls. There was an impressive looking hob and three enormous ovens along one side of the large room, as well as a huge refrigerator.

"I love this kitchen, Mr Steiner," she breathed.

Mr Steiner did not want to be rude to Maddie – after all she had been very good to him on Saturday – but he did not want her here.

She hopped on the stool he'd just vacated and said. "Sometimes I used to sit on this stool and watch Mrs Steiner ice her cinnamon buns. She said they were the only thing she could bake better than you. And she'd let me have one."

Mr Steiner blinked back tears, turning away before the child could see them. The vision of his wife, icing buns while Maddie nattered away beside her, brought the tears but it also softened him. He gathered his control and turned back to Maddie, smiling.

"She did make the best cinnamon buns," he said. "I suppose I was at Oompah practise when you did this?"

"Yes," Maddie agreed. She giggled. "But I always thought she said 'jumper' band. I imagined you all wearing big woolly jumpers."

Mr Steiner smiled. "*Nein,*" he said. "I wanted us to wear *lederhosen* but nobody else would."

"What's that?" Maddie asked.

"*Lederhosen*? Short leather trousers with braces." Mr Steiner mimed twanging the braces.

"Wouldn't they look silly?" Maddie laughed.

Mr Steiner shook his head. "Not on an Oompah band. That is traditional Bavarian dress."

"What's 'Bavarian'?"

"It's a part of Germany," Mr Steiner explained. "It is where I originally come from."

"That's why you talk funny," Maddie nodded sagely.

Mr Steiner couldn't help smiling. "Maybe it is you that talk funny."

"But I talk like everyone else," Maddie said.

"Then you all talk funny."

"Noooooo," Maddie laughed.

Mr Steiner found he liked her laugh. It was tinklingly infectious. But, he reminded himself, he had far too much to do to stand here chatting. And what would her mother think to know Maddie was alone with a man she didn't know very well? It wasn't the sort of thing people did anymore, what with all the awful headlines in the news.

"Does your mother know you're here?" he asked.

"Mum's working," Maddie said. "Nanny Dot knows. She's coming around in a bit."

This was a surprise. "She is? Why?"

"So I can help you bake," Maddie said, as though it was perfectly obvious.

Mr Steiner frowned. "Maddie, I'm too busy to help you bake today."

"No," Maddie said patiently. "I'm helping you to bake."

Ach du lieber! This child. How would Betty handle the situation? "That is not possible," Mr Steiner said gently. "I have too much to do."

"Yes," Maddie said. "That's why I'll help."

Lieber Gott! Mr Steiner thought. She was like chewing gum on a pavement – very hard to remove.

Maddie waved past him to the door. Mr Steiner turned to see Maddie's grandmother peering in. She grinned and pushed her way in, bearing a large bulging carrier bag and a black leather case. The kitchen was very big but it suddenly felt small to Mr Steiner.

"Yoo hoo," Mrs Flowers said. "I've brought some CDs to play." She crossed to the workbench and much to Mr Steiner's horror laid the leather case on it. He kept his baking surfaces clean and sterile and now this woman was dumping her dirty stuff on it willy-nilly.

"What's that?" Maddie asked, leaning over to examine the case.

Mrs Flowers unlatched it. The hinges creaked as it opened to reveal a dull silver trumpet.

Maddie caught her breath. "Your trumpet!"

"And my old cleaning kit," Mrs Flowers pointed to the various odd-looking brushes and bottles nestled next to the instrument. "I'm not sure how much good that will be after so many years but I'll try giving it a clean-up while you help Mr Steiner."

Mr Steiner couldn't hold back any longer. "That is it!" he declared. "Mrs Flowers, I am a very busy man. You *und* Madeleine cannot stay. I am very grateful for Maddie's help on Saturday but a dangerous kitchen is no place for a little girl. *Und* I am behind with my baking."

He saw the disappointment on Maddie's face and tried to harden his heart against it. Really, could they not see he had a job to do?

Mrs Flower's face creased in concern. Her eyes were kind – certainly kinder than they had been on Saturday. "Mr Steiner," she said quietly, taking his arm. "Can I have a quick word?"

Before he knew it Mr Steiner had been steered into the passage between the kitchen and the shop and manoeuvred so that both he and Mrs Flowers had their backs to Maddie.

"I'm sorry to do this, Mr Steiner," Mrs Flowers said, keeping her voice low so that he had to lean in to hear her. "But Maddie is having a difficult time at the moment."

"Oh, yes?"

"It's the snow," Mrs Flowers whispered. "I don't know if you remember but Maddie's father went missing in the snow."

Truth be told Mr Steiner had forgotten. It had been years ago but now he'd been reminded he could vividly remember joining the search party organised two days after he'd gone missing. Privately he'd always assumed Vincent Larkin had done a runner, leaving his wife with a new baby and a broken heart but good-hearted Betty said Vincent was a lovely young man, besotted by his tiny daughter, and she didn't think he could do such a thing. But then Betty always saw the good in people while he often looked for the bad.

He felt ashamed for forgetting. "I remember," he nodded at Mrs Flowers.

"Maddie hates the snow," Mrs Flowers explained. "It makes her feel sad and it's much worse this year."

"It is very much like that winter," Mr Steiner agreed.

"But working with you on Saturday really took her mind off it," Mrs Flowers said. "She'd talked of nothing else. And she really does miss Betty too. I know it's a lot to ask but if you could let her help it would make her so happy."

Mr Steiner was in a fix. He really didn't want to be bothered. How would he ever get all his baking done with a little girl getting in his way? And he resented Mrs Flowers for her persuasive argument. It would make him feel awfully mean if he turned them away.

What would Betty do, he asked himself.

Mr Steiner sighed. The answer was obvious. "Very well," he said. "But Maddie must do exactly what I say."

"She will," Mrs Flowers said, breaking into a beatific smile. "Thank you, Mr Steiner."

He gave her a curt nod and turned back to the kitchen where Maddie was waiting expectantly.

"You will need an apron and to tie back your hair and you must wash your hands thoroughly," he said to her.

"Yippee!" Maddie cried, hopping off the stool. "Thank you, Mr Steiner."

Half an hour later Mr Steiner was teaching Maddie to use the cookie press.

"This is awesome," Maddie exclaimed pushing the spritz cookie dough into the tube.

"Awesome," Mr Steiner repeated. "What a strange thing to say."

From the corner Mrs Flowers looked up from cleaning her trumpet and rolled her eyes at him. "Oh, they all say it. This is awesome, that's awesome. They haven't a clue what it really means."

"What does it mean then?" Maddie said, tamping down her dough. "I think it means 'really great'."

"It sort of does," Mrs Flowers agreed. "But more so…"

"It means to be in awe of something," Mr Steiner explained. "To find it almost terrible in its overwhelming beauty. In German we say '*ehrfurcht vor jdm. haben*', meaning to 'have reverence for'."

"Isn't that religious?" Maddie asked. "We study religion at school but we're not religious, are we Nanny?"

"No, we're not," Mrs Flowers agreed. "But I do have 'reverence' for lots of things that are wonderful."

"*Ja*," Mr Steiner agreed. "*Und* the cookie press is not one of them. It is not 'awesome'. The mountains covered in snow in the Bavarian Alps are 'awesome'. The cookie press, not so."

Maddie was quiet as he guided her to press down on the cookie press lever. She gasped as the snowflake shape cookies emerged. "No," she said. "You're wrong. The cookie press is definitely 'awesome'!"

Mr Steiner laughed. He couldn't stop himself giving her shoulders an affectionate squeeze and was shocked to realize just how long it was since he'd hugged anyone. Or they him.

#

They baked and baked and baked while the snow fell outside and the afternoon faded towards evening.

Maddie learnt how to make German gingerbread. She weighed out the ingredients for stollen under Mr Steiner's specific instructions and watched him mix it in his industrial size dough mixer until it came out in a massive, sticky ball which he smacked down onto the floured bench and set to beating it up.

"What are you doing?" Maddie asked. This was possibly her two hundredth question of the afternoon.

"It is called kneading," Mr Steiner said, rolling the dough back towards him before pushing it vigorously away with the heel of his hands, all the while folding it. "Stollen is a type of bread dough. Kneading the dough helps develop the gluten from the flour and water and spread the gas around from the yeast. *Unterstandt, ja*?"

Maddie shook her head. "No."

"It makes the bread texture *gut* and light, not heavy and dense."

"Ah!" Maddie says. "Mum made bread once. Nanny Dot said she could sell the recipe to make house bricks."

"*Das* is funny!" Mr Steiner smiled.

"Your mother's not been blessed with the baking gene," Nanny Dot said, peering down the funnel of her trumpet. "She's a good home-cook though."

"Her meals are yummy," Maddie agreed. "Except the one with liver and lentils." She stuck her tongue out. "That's yucky."

Mr Steiner oiled the sides of a large bowl and dumped the dough into it. "Now we will let that rise for a couple of hours in the proofing oven."

"A couple of hours!" Maddie gasped. "It takes so long to bake?"

Mr Steiner smiled wryly. "Not bake, Madeleine. The dough must rise…" He mimicked swelling up, puffing out his chest and cheeks. "And then it must be kneaded again *und* filled with marzipan und put into smaller loaf tins to bake."

"That's so much work," Maddie said, dismayed. "It doesn't take long to eat."

"*Ja*," Mr Steiner agreed. "Thank goodness it is only made at Christmas time." He carried the enormous bowl to his proofing oven and slid it in.

A knock sounded at the door causing them all to jump. The door opened and Mum stuck her head in. "Hello?" she said. "Can I come in?"

"Mum," Maddie cried. "Look at all the things we've made."

"Wow," Mum said, gazing at the numerous trays of cooling cookies, gingerbread and other scrumptious treats. "It smells wonderful in here."

"*Wunderbar*," Maddie corrected her. She pronounced the 'w' as a 'vee' sound the way Mr Steiner did. "It's German for wonderful. Right, Mr Steiner?"

"*Ja,*" Mr Steiner said. "*Wunderbar. Das ist richtig.* That is right."

Maddie beamed at him.

"How was the shop today?" Nanny Dot asked Mum.

"Busy," Mum sighed. "I'm shattered but Sally is a huge help. It's snowing like mad again. At this rate everyone will be staying in for the rest of the week."

Maddie grimaced. "I wish it would stop." She felt Mr Steiner's kind hand on her shoulder.

"Don't worry," he said. "When I was a boy in Bavaria this would be considered a mild winter."

"Really?"

"Really."

"I'm sure Mr Steiner's had enough of you for the day, Maddie," Mum said. "She can talk the hind leg off a donkey," she added to Mr Steiner.

"She has been delightful," Mr Steiner defended Maddie. "*Und* this donkey still has his hind legs."

Nanny Dot guffawed. "I've never understood that expression," she said. "We'll be along in half an hour, Lily. Maddie can help Mr Steiner clean up."

Mr Steiner waved the suggestion away. "No need. I'll be working for hours yet. *Und* I clean as I go."

It was true. Mr Steiner was extremely efficient, loading the dishwasher as he went, or hand washing some items that were delicate or he needed again. He kept the work tops wiped down after each task was completed.

"But I want to ice some cookies," Maddie said.

"I doubt you'll be able to do them to Mr Steiner's standard," Mum warned. "Remember, Mr Steiner has to sell them."

"She can do a few," Mr Steiner said.

"Okay," Mum agreed, "but be home in an hour. Tea will be on the table for six thirty." She looked at Mr Steiner. "Are you sure you don't mind?"

"Not at all."

Mum looked unconvinced. "You eating with us Mum?" she asked Nanny Dot.

"Please, " Nanny Dot said. "I'll bring Maddie home soon."

Mum suddenly noticed what Nanny was doing. "Your trumpet! It's been years since I've seen that."

Nanny nodded. "I'll tell you about it later," she said, polishing up the metal till it gleamed.

"Can Mum have this gingerbread?" Maddie begged Mr Steiner. "It's a bit wonky."

"Of course," Mr Steiner said.

Maddie pushed the gingerbread into Mum's hand. "Me and Mr Steiner made it."

"I'll have it with a cup of tea," Mum said. "I need to put my feet up for ten minutes. I'm worn out."

Once Mum had gone, Maddie exchanged a significant look with Nanny Dot. They were thinking the same thing: what effect would the gingerbread have on Mum?

5

The effect of the gingerbread on Mum was magic.

Maddie and Nanny Dot opened the flat door to the sound of Mum singing 'Joy to the World' at the top of her voice.

They found her in the kitchen mashing potato for a shepherd's pie with a vigour she didn't usually have after a long day in the flower shop.

"Goodness," Nanny said. "You sound happy."

"I know!" Mum grinned. "I feel like a new woman. After a cup of tea and the gingerbread – delicious Maddie - I had a little snooze. It did me the world of good, I must say."

Maddie excitedly nudged Nanny.

"How did the icing go?" Mum asked.

"I need a lot of practise," Maddie admitted. "Mr Steiner's were much better."

"Well, he's been doing it for years," Mum said. She artfully spread the mash over the top of her shepherd's pie, making pretty rills in it with a fork and held the large dish up for them to admire before she slid it into the oven.

"You know, this is the first time I've genuinely felt Christmassy this year," Mum admitted.

That was another thing about adults Maddie didn't understand. She'd overheard various adults over the years say they just couldn't feel Christmassy. How could you not feel it? She fervently hoped that wouldn't happen to her when she grew up. What an awful thought.

"I felt bad leaving Mr Steiner," Maddie said. "He still has lots to do. Maybe I can go back after tea?"

"Surely he's having a break?" Mum said.

Nanny replied. "I get the impression he forgets to eat. Have you noticed how thin he's become?"

"Oh dear," Mum said. "I hadn't noticed. In fact, when I think about it I've hardly spoken to him all year. It was Betty I used to chat to." She looked guilty.

"Mum," she said to Nanny. "Go back and ask him to tea. There's enough for all of us. Make him come, if only for half an hour; insist if you have to."

Maddie stared at her mum. This was so unlike her. Mum was friendly with her customers and had a couple of pals she met for coffee twice a month but she didn't spontaneously invite people for tea, not even Daisy and Suzy. It all had to be planned in advance. She was acting more like Nanny.

Nanny returned with Mr Steiner reluctantly in tow.

"This is too kind," he said, wringing his hands as he stood awkwardly in the doorway. "I would not impose but your mother is very…"

"Bossy," Mum laughed.

"I was going to say 'persuasive'," Mr Steiner blushed.

"I prefer yours," Nanny Dot said to Mr Steiner.

"I like Mum's better," Maddie said, dodging a playful swat from Nanny.

"Cheeky monkey."

"C'mon, Mr Steiner," Maddie said, grabbing his hand. "I'll show you the tree."

They ate tea at the kitchen table. Mum's shepherd's pie was extra delicious.

"You are a very good cook," Mr Steiner told her, making Mum flush with pleasure.

"What's for afters?" Maddie asked.

"I brought a stollen I made yesterday," Mr Steiner said. "It was one of the few things I didn't ruin."

Mum's eyes lit up.

Maddie looked at Nanny in panic. Anything Mr Steiner had made yesterday would make them feel sad.

"Oh no," Maddie said, thinking quickly. "We can't have that, Mr Steiner. You need it to sell. You said you're behind with your baking."

"That's right," Nanny added. "You've worked too hard to waste it on us. Let's have ice cream instead."

Mum looked disappointed but she valiantly said. "They're right. You put it in the shop."

"Thank you," Mr Steiner said. "That reminds me. I really must get back or I won't have enough for tomorrow."

"Oh, please have some ice-cream, Mr Steiner," Maddie cried. She was enjoying having four of them around the table.

Mr Steiner shook his head. "I'm afraid I've lost my taste for sweet things since my Bettina died."

"But you're a baker," Maddie exclaimed. "Don't you eat your cakes and biscuits?"

"No," Mr Steiner said sadly. "I know the recipes so well I don't bother to taste them anymore. Betty was my main taster. I'm afraid…" he stumbled over his words. "I'm afraid that was why her heart was weak. Too much fat. Too much sugar."

Maddie was dismayed to see him on the verge of tears again.

Nanny Dot reached over and put her hand over Mr Steiner's. "My Fred died of a heart attack," she said. "He was only forty two, cycled to work every day, and never touched a scrap of fat. Sometimes these things just happen."

"Forty two!" Mr Steiner said. "So young." He looked at Nanny Dot with sympathy and squeezed her hand back. "I forget it isn't just me."

"No, it isn't," Nanny agreed. "Any time you want to talk about Betty, Mr Steiner, you can talk to me. I remember how it is when you lose a loved one.

Suddenly people are embarrassed to speak of them to you and it's like losing them all over again."

"Thank you," Mr Steiner said. "*Und* please, call me Hans."

"Why are people embarrassed?" Maddie asked. "I like to remember Mrs Steiner."

Nanny smiled. "They think if they mention the person you've lost it will hurt you, I suppose. But in the end that starts to hurt more."

Maddie digested this. In a quiet voice she said. "It hurts me that we don't talk about Dad."

There was a shocked silence at the table. Finally Mum got up and started to clear the dishes away. Trying to smile, she said: "Now, who's for ice-cream?"

"Show me the tree again, Maddie," Mr Steiner said.

Maddie thought it an odd request but politely led him back to the lounge. There Mr Steiner leaned down to her and whispered. "I don't know much about your father, Madeleine, but I know my Betty liked him very much. She didn't believe he left you on purpose."

"I think he left because of me," Maddie whispered back. "Maybe I was bad. I know I cried a lot as a baby."

Mr Steiner smiled kindly. "All babies cry a lot. But I know you're not a bad girl, otherwise the Krampus would have got you by now."

"What's a 'Krampus'?" Maddie asked.

"Ah, now," Mr Steiner said straightening up and going over to the armchair by the fire. "The Krampus is a hideous creature that punishes bad boys and girls at Christmas time in Bavaria. He travels with Saint Nicholas."

"Santa Claus?"

"Like him."

"Tell me," Maddie begged. "Tell me about the Krampus."

"All right," Mr Steiner said, settling back into his chair while Maddie flopped down at his feet. "I will tell you."

Mum and Nanny came in and settled on the sofa.

"When I was a little boy in Bavaria…" Mr Steiner began.

#

When Mr Steiner was a little boy in Bavaria, the Krampus returned to his small town at the foot of the Alps after years of being banished by the Nazi party who ruled Germany and Austria and other European countries up to the end of the Second World War. Mr Steiner was born in the years after the war. Nobody wanted to talk about the Nazis in those times, but gradually things that had been part of German life before the Nazis' reign made their way back into people's lives.

The Krampus was one of them and he scared the socks off little Hans Steiner because the Krampus is a demon. The strange thing is he's a great pal of St Nicholas, who's a bit like Santa Claus but instead of visiting on Christmas Eve, St Nick visits the children of Bavaria on the evening of December fifth to leave them small presents – often in their shoes – to find the next morning.

The Krampus comes with him. Or sometimes he comes on his own. But he always comes.

He is fearsome in appearance with the arms and chest of a man and the legs of a goat, deep furred all over with burning crimson eyes and long curling horns. Worst is his tongue; blood red and pointed and oh, so very long, it writhes between dagger teeth that could tear a child in two.

In fact, his favourite meal is child and he carries a tub on his back to steal away the very naughtiest children to his lair.

For it is naughty children he is interested in. Most of the time he simply whips them with his birch stick, or drags them out of their warm house to dump them in the snow. A child must have been very bad indeed to be stolen away. The Krampus always knows who they are.

Little Hans Steiner had older twin brothers, Pieter and Udo. They teased him mercilessly, shoved snow down inside his vest, trapped him down the bottom of his bedclothes until he could hardly breathe but their very favourite form of torture to inflict on poor Hans was for one of them to hold him down while the other sat over his face and trumped.

Pieter's most beloved toy was an automaton monkey that played a small accordion, while Udo's was a clockwork tin motorcycle complete with sidecar and riders. These shared a special space on the shelf in the twins' bedroom and Hans was forbidden to ever touch them or even to go into their room.

One day, after Pieter and Udo rolled Hans into a giant snowball and sent him spinning down a hill, Hans had had enough. Once he'd broken out of his ice prison and trudged back up the hill in sopping wet clothes to home, he discovered Pieter and Hans already dry and warm in front of the fire.

"Oh Hans," his mother groaned when she saw the state of him. "Why must you always make such a mess of yourself?"

The blood in Han's veins boiled with the injustice of this. His mother had a blind spot when it came to the twins; with their angelic faces, blue eyes and white-blond hair they looked like Christmas angels. There was no point in trying to place the blame on them, no matter how much they deserved it.

The twins grinned wickedly at him from behind their mother's back and thumbed their noses.

"Look at you," Mama said. "You have torn your trousers you naughty boy. If you carry on like this the Krampus will get you."

A year ago perhaps, certainly two, this statement would have struck fear into Hans's heart but at nine, he wasn't so sure he believed in the Krampus anymore.

After all, no one was naughtier than the twins and yet the Krampus had never come for them.

Still, the mention of the Krampus gave him an idea and the seeds of his revenge began to sprout in Hans's mind.

Before school Hans often went to work in his father's bakery, helping him to bake for the coming day. It meant rising very early, especially hard on dark, cold winter mornings, but Hans didn't mind. He loved the bakery, warm and fragrant, as well as the feel of dough in his hands. He liked to plunge his fingers into sacks of powdery flour, grate pungent nutmeg into a mixture, or beat the grit of sugar into butter until it was as smooth and silken as his mother's face cream.

Neither of the twins had inherited their father's baking skills. They preferred the rough and tumble of the outdoors, feeding the chickens and the pigs, milking the cow, chopping the wood. And of course, torturing Hans. Han's father loved all his boys, but unlike his wife he wasn't blind to the mischief the twins liked to cause or to the way they teased Hans. Whereas Hans had inherited his natural aptitude for baking, Mr Steiner had passed on his dazzling angelic looks to the twins, and he knew from personal experience that it allowed them to get away with far more than they should, not just at home but at school too.

So, while he never favoured any of the boys outwardly, Hans could sense his father's understanding and felt happy working alongside him.

On the morning of December the fifth, three days after Hans had been rolled down the hill in a giant snowball, Mr Steiner found him already in the kitchen, cutting festive shapes out of salt dough.

"What are you doing?"

"Mrs Schmidt asked me to make some salt-dough decorations for the classroom," Hans said. "I thought I could bake them with the bread before I go to school. We'll paint them in class."

"That's a fine idea," his father said.

Salt dough wasn't for eating. It would bake rock hard into whatever shape you chose and wouldn't turn soft with paint, so it was perfect for making decorations, yet Hans wasn't being strictly truthful with his father.

True, he had cut out some stars and angel shapes to take to school, but his main achievement of the morning had been to make a pair of wicked looking Krampus claws and a pair of cloven hooves. Both pairs were made from dough and he'd painstakingly moulded and crafted them, using a stick to make holes in the claws and a stilt end for the hooves. These were hidden on a baking tray at the bottom of the oven and Hans hoped he could slip them out without his father seeing.

He'd had to get up so early to secretly make them that by mid-morning Mrs Schmidt rapped him sharply with a ruler because he'd fallen asleep during arithmetic, but it was worth it, knowing that tonight – Krampusnacht - he would execute his revenge on his brothers.

All the children were excited and fearful because by the following morning Saint Nicholas might leave a gift – if they'd been good – or if they were bad the Krampus might come for them. Sleep took a long time to take hold. In bedrooms all over town parents were saying 'just go to sleep' for the fifth or sixth time.

For Hans the opposite was true as he had to fight to stay awake longer than the twins. His mother and father had to hush them seven times before peace finally fell and the house creaked comfortably into a doze.

Hans waited until he was sure everyone was asleep, including his parents, before he pushed back his bedclothes and rose, still fully dressed. He crossed to the wardrobe and opened it as quietly as he could, grimacing as the hinges squeaked. Holding his breath, Hans listened, but nothing else stirred so he pushed through his clothes to the back of the wardrobe where he'd hidden his props. One by one he took them out. Moonlight shone through the window, illuminating the strange articles. Earlier, he'd smuggled a pot of glue out of art class – when they'd been painting the salt dough baubles – and barricaded himself in his bedroom to get to work on his project.

First, he'd poured a little glue into the holes he'd left in the Krampus's clawed hands and then slotted two long, straightish sticks he'd made out of branches into the holes. He left them to set while he did the same with the Krampus hooves. This time he inserted a pair of stilts into the hooves. They were the stilts he'd had from Saint Nicholas last year, the same day that the twins had received their marvellous presents of the accordion-playing monkey and the clockwork motorcycle.

It was his own fault he'd got stilts, he supposed, as he'd been so taken by a stilt-walker when a carnival had come to town, that he'd spent that autumn talking about little else.

The twins had jeered at his stilts and, of course, taken to knocking him off them whenever they caught him practising, so that Hans came to resent them and wished he'd had a wonderful clockwork toy instead.

Now he was very, very glad to have his stilts, and gladder still to have mastered them.

In the moonlit room Hans completed the final touches; he dusted the palms of his Krampus claws with coal dust and did the underside of the hooves. Lastly he picked up the moth-eaten fox fur his mother never wore but wouldn't throw out (he'd raided her wardrobe for that) and snipped off patches of hair.

He was ready.

Quietly Hans slipped out of his room and crept downstairs, awkwardly carrying his props, grateful for the moon shining its cold light through a thin window at the top of the landing so he could see his way. The locks on the back door seemed as loud as gunshots as he slid them back. Again, he paused to listen, but thankfully no one stirred.

The cold was biting outside but Hans was hot with excitement and fear. He stepped onto his stilts and prayed the glue would hold and the salt dough hooves wouldn't crumple beneath his weight.

The glue held and so did the Krampus hooves.

Gingerly, Hans took his first stilted step on the snow, and then the next. It was difficult because as well as having to hold onto the top of the stilt poles he had to carry his Krampus claws. Luckily Hans was a bright boy and had already solved the problem by tying the sticks to his wrists. It was clumsy as they knocked against the stilts but it worked.

Hans set off around the back of the house. The first time he didn't stop below his brothers' window but kept on going in a circle right back to where he'd started. He reversed direction and took the opposite way round the house and this time he did stop under their window. He was gratified to see his paired hoof prints clearly leaving sooty marks in the snow. It looked as though the Krampus had gone all round the house looking for the twins' room.

Leaning himself against the wall, Hans carefully lifted his long sticks until they reached the sill of the window above and placed the Krampus claws in the snow nestled there. Gently he tapped the claws against the glass but not hard enough to make a sound – or so he hoped – because he didn't want to wake the boys, just make prints on the windowpane. It was tricky to do because maintaining control of the sticks above his head whilst leaning against the wall on stilts was extremely difficult, but Hans managed it.

Finally he sprinkled the fox fur on the ground, to make it seem as though the Krampus had shed some of his hideous hide, and set off for the back door.

Slipping inside, Hans relocked the door and crept back upstairs. Inside his room he stowed the stilts and sticks inside his wardrobe, sighing with relief that the first part of the plan had gone so well.

The second part was riskier.

Once more he tiptoed onto the landing, this time turning towards his brothers' room.

Their door was ajar as his mother insisted that with the two of them sharing the room there wasn't enough air for both of them unless either the door or the window was open. This was not the weather for opening the window.

Tentatively, Hans entered the twins' room.

Udo was snoring while Pieter breathed deeply and slowly, a sure sign both were asleep.

Silently, Hans crossed to the shelf where they kept the monkey and the motorcycle, taking one in each hand.

Udo turned over, muttering, making Hans freeze in place until Udo began to snore again.

Hans stole to the door and slipped out onto the landing which was part flooded in moonlight, part deep in shadow.

In the shadow something stirred; something large, with wickedly curved horns and claws for hands.

Hans let out a high yelp. The Krampus!

"Shhh," the creature rasped. "Quiet boy. What have you there?"

Trembling, Hans held up his brothers' prized toys.

The Krampus remained mostly hidden in the shadow but it reached out a claw on the end of a furred arm and pointed at Hans.

"Do you want to reconsider?" it growled, "and put them back."

Hans nodded his head vigorously. Yes. Yes he did. He inched back into his brothers' room, almost tripped over the rug but just managed to right himself, and returned the toys to their shelf.

Facing the landing and the beast again was perhaps the bravest thing Hans ever did.

It was still there, lurking, and while Hans couldn't see its eyes he knew they burnt with the red fires of Hell, just like the legend said.

"To bed," the Krampus commanded. "Before I change my mind and take you for my supper. And," it lowered its horrible voice into a gravelly whisper. "Whatever you may hear, do not get out of bed. Understand?"

Hans did understand. His nerve broke and he bolted for his bedroom. Jumping into bed, he yanked the covers over his head and jammed a finger in each ear.

He thought he'd never be able to sleep ever again, but that wasn't true. Sometime after three o' clock he drifted away only to be awakened at first light by a commotion from his brothers' room.

What a clamour they made. "Mama, Mama!"

Hans heard his mother run from her room to see what the fuss was about.

"Udo, Pieter, whatever is it?"

Hans peeped out. His father, still in his pyjamas, hurried past. Hans followed him.

The twins' faces were pale, their cheeks stained with tears.

"Oh Mama," Udo said. "The Krampus came. He woke us in the night…"

"He had horns this big," Pieter said, holding his arms as far apart as he could.

"And eyes of fire."

"And terrible fur."

"He stole our toys."

"And he told us we had to be nice to…" At this Udo nudged Pieter to shut him up but both boys were looking at Hans begrudgingly.

"Nonsense," their mother said crossly. "You are far too old to believe in the Krampus."

"But's it true, Mama," Udo said, breaking into tears. "Look what he left us." He pointed at the shelf. Where the monkey and the motorcycle had been, there were two lumps of coal instead.

Mama gasped and looked sharply at her husband but he was staring at the windowpane.

"Look at this," he said, peering closely. There was a distinct, sooty claw mark imprinted on the glass.

They all crowded round the window.

"Look," Pieter shouted. "They're on the windowsill too."

Sure enough they were. Udo hoisted the window to lean out. The snow below was littered with cloven hoof prints.

"See Mama," the twins' wailed. "We told you so. The Krampus has been."

"Rubbish," Mrs Steiner snapped. "It is a joke, that's all." Again she narrowed her eyes at her husband suspiciously.

"Don't you look at me that way, Mama Steiner," Mr Steiner said. "It wasn't me. And if the twins' say they saw him, well then who am I to say they didn't?"

"And what about you?" Mrs Steiner turned on Hans. "I suppose you saw him too?"

Before he could reply, Udo sneered. "Oh, Hans is too much of a goody-two -shoes for the Krampus to bother with."

Pieter gave his brother a swipe to the head and glared at him.

"What?!" Udo protested but then he caught the meaning behind his brother's glare and reddened. He added politely. "Er, I mean, it's good Hans didn't see him. Lucky you, Hans."

"I suppose this means we won't have any presents from Saint Nicholas," Pieter said miserably.

Mr and Mrs Steiner exchanged a smile.

"Why don't we go and see?"

In the hallway downstairs each boy had left a pair of boots for Saint Nicholas to fill.

The twins' reached theirs first, eyes lighting up.

"Oh wow," Udo said, fishing a bag of chocolates from his, as well as a new pocketknife.

Pieter got the same.

Hans also had chocolate. Underneath that was a beautiful clockwork fire engine with a fireman who ran up and down a ladder.

Hans gazed at it in pure delight. It was as marvellous as the automaton monkey and the clockwork motorbike.

Suddenly he felt sorry for his brothers. Theirs had been exchanged for lumps of coal by the Krampus. He was glad now that it wasn't him who had taken their toys.

"What's that?" Mama said, pointing to a cardboard box nearby. "It has the twins' name on it."

Puzzled, she handed the box to Udo who opened it. Inside were the monkey and the motorbike. On top of them lay a note.

Udo read it aloud: **Dear Udo and Pieter, you are very lucky boys. I have just met the Krampus coming out of your house and persuaded him to give you one more chance to mend your ways.**

However take this as warning. The Krampus does not like to lose. He says that if you don't keep to your promise, next time he won't just take the

toys; he will take you both as well and have you for his supper.

I will not interfere on your behalf again, so take heed: Beware the Krampus. He always knows what you do.

Yours, Saint Nicholas.

The twins' shuddered along with Hans.

"What did you promise?" Hans asked them.

Both boys looked at him oddly. "We're not allowed to say," Udo muttered. "That was part of the promise."

The three boys couldn't resist checking the toe of their boot for any missed present but only Hans found something in the bottom of his. He drew it out carefully.

He and his family stared at it for a moment. It was another lump of coal.

"Ha!" Udo began to laugh. "It looks like we're all in it together."

And after their visit from the Krampus they were.

#

"He made them promise to be nice to you, didn't he?" Maddie said, wide-eyed.

"*Ja*," Mr Steiner said. "Things got better after that."

"The Krampus is real then," Maddie said with a shiver. She felt both thrilled and scared.

"Er, no," her mother said. "It's just a story Mr Steiner's made up to entertain us." She gave Mr Steiner a warning look.

"*Nein.*" Mr Steiner shook his head. "It happened exactly as I said." He leaned forward. "But as I got older I realised it was not the Krampus who came but more likely my father dressed up as him."

"No!" cried Maddie. "I think it was the Krampus. You *saw* him."

"I was a scared little boy who saw him in the shadows. I made Krampus claws, so could have my father. My mother had a fur coat. He could have made his horns – maybe out of salt dough as I made my hooves."

"But why would your father bother?" Maddie asked.

Mr Steiner smiled. "*Acht*, my father was a clever man. He knew if he told my brothers to leave me alone it would only make them worse. They would think I was his favourite. But if it came from the Krampus…"

"They'd be too scared not to," Maddie nodded.

"Yes," Nanny Dot joined in. "And by giving you a lump of coal too, they'd think the Krampus was sending you a warning and not resent you."

"*Ja*," Mr Steiner agreed. "*Und* I think my father was telling me the Krampus had not forgotten my bad behaviour that night."

"Did it work?" Mum asked.

"Oh *ja*! I was terrified of the Krampus for years and so were my brothers. They were much nicer to me after that night *und* we became closer as we got older."

"Are you still friends?" Maddie asked.

Mr Steiner thought about this. He looked a little sad. "*Ja*, but I don't talk to them as much as I should do." He brightened. "I will call them on Christmas day, I think."

He stood. "I have to get on with my baking, but thank you so much for tea. It has been a pleasure."

"It was our pleasure," Mum said warmly.

"I could help you in the shop tomorrow," Nanny Dot offered.

Mr Steiner looked like he was about to refuse.

"Oh yes, please. Can we?" Maddie begged.

He gave in. "Thank you. It would be a big help."

Mum saw him out.

Maddie's heart raced. She didn't believe it was Mr Steiner's father he had seen. She thought the Krampus really had helped him out, and if the Krampus was real – terrifying though he could be – perhaps all sorts of other unlikely things could be true too.

Like magical baking.

Or long-lost fathers coming home.

The Krampus wasn't the only thing on Maddie's mind that evening. She'd done something naughty earlier and was planning to do an even naughtier thing later on that night.

Seeing the effect of the gingerbread on Mum's mood made her more determined to do it, although it was risky. In fact it was illegal.

Maddie intended to commit burglary.

She had lifted the spare key to the bakery kitchen off a peg in Mr Steiner's pantry when he wasn't looking.

She knew it was the spare key because Mrs Steiner had once told her so. She kept it there after Mr Steiner had once accidentally locked her in the kitchen. Mrs Steiner had been rootling in the pantry, but he thought she'd already gone upstairs to their flat. He locked the interior door between the shop and the bakery and went off whistling. Poor old Mrs Steiner was locked in for two hours before he came back, and this was in the days before mobile phones.

The reason behind Maddie's intended burglary was simple. She was going to steal the 'sad' baked goods that Mr Steiner had made yesterday. He said he hadn't managed to make many worth selling, but there were some – the stollen he'd brought round for dessert was one. Maddie couldn't bear the idea of customers who ate them becoming miserable so close to Christmas, or even worse on Christmas day if they saved the treats for then.

Now she had proof that Mr Steiner's baking had a magical effect, Maddie felt it was her duty to get rid of the bad stuff.

She and Nanny had cheered Mr Steiner up and it had spread into his baking. Mum's good mood was proof of that. If they could keep it up think how happy Christmas would be for the people who ate his goods Just the thought of it gave her a glow.

She supposed she could have asked Mr Steiner not to sell yesterday's goods but then she'd have to tell him why. He wouldn't believe her. Most adults wouldn't. Nanny Dot was an exception. And even if he did believe her he'd know his lovely-tasting treats had made people feel horrible and then he'd feel sad about that. Now Maddie knew how nice Mr Steiner was she couldn't do that to him..

No, she would sneak in the bakery tonight, swipe them, and throw them away. She wasn't going to tell Nanny Dot what she was going to do because even Nanny Dot was too much of a grown up to approve of burglary, whatever the reason.

Her mind bubbled with excitement and she could hardly concentrate on watching Elf with Nanny and Mum, although it was her favourite Christmas film ever.

As soon as it was over she faked a huge yawn and said she was going to bed just so she could be alone in her room to think her plan through.

The hours seemed endless until Mum and Nanny Dot went to bed. She could hear them nattering and laughing, rustling paper (wrapping presents!?) and moving around in the flat. Finally she heard the familiar metal slide of the sofa bed being pulled out for Nanny and heard Mum go into her bathroom to take off her make-up and clean her teeth.

She thought about nine year old Hans Steiner waiting for his family to go to sleep but quickly forced the thought away. If she thought about the Krampus she'd never have the courage to go out in the dark.

Mum opened her door and came in. Maddie, fully clothed under the covers, pretended to be asleep.

"Night, night darling," Mum whispered, planting a petal-soft kiss on Maddie's brow before tiptoeing out of the room.

How could time move so slowly? Maddie sighed as she forced herself to wait until she was sure her mother and Nanny Dot must be asleep.

There was no moonlight, as there had been for Hans Steiner, but when Maddie opened her bedroom curtains there was plenty of light to see by. It had stopped snowing but the streetlights bounced eerily off the whiteness and into Maddie's room.

Getting out of the flat without waking Mum would normally be impossible, but Mum said she slept better with Nanny Dot staying. She said if anyone broke in they'd get Nanny Dot first or Nanny would get them.

Maddie crept past her mum's room, and the lounge, in her woolly socks. She pulled on her wellies, quietly slid the bolts back, and turned her key in the squeaky lock.

Eeek. It sounded like a mouse – a very big, noisy mouse – and Maddie tensed, waiting for either Mum or Nanny or both to wake up and demand to know what she was doing.

Neither did. Letting out her breath she slipped through the door and down the stairs to the front door that opened onto their drive.

The night was still, the air freezing. Maddie crunched through the fresh snow to the bakery. Bins lined the street waiting for the last collection before Christmas.

The passageway to the kitchen door looked as black as the space under Maddie's bed. She would have to enter this blackness to reach the kitchen door.

But Maddie was a resourceful girl and came prepared. She took a torch from her pocket and shone the beam into the dark entry. The first half of the alley, at least, was empty.

Maddie took a deep breath and forced herself forward, waving the torch in front of her like a sword. No, Maddie, thought. Not like a sword. Like a laser-gun, and if anything horrible tried to attack she would blast them with it.

The shadows retreated before her until she reached the kitchen door. An outside lamp over the door came on, triggered by her movement, flooding the alley in light. Maddie gasped, caught in the act. Nervously, she looked back at the street, thinking someone might have seen the light, but no one was around.

Maddie turned her attention back to the job. Here was the moment. She had stolen the key and now she was going to use it.

Maddie Larkin. Thief.

With trembling fingers, Maddie fitted the key to the lock and turned it. She heard the tumblers spring and pushed the door open.

Now, Maddie was lucky; if she had unlocked the door to the shop itself, outer door or inner door, she would have set off a racket to wake the town, but it had never occurred to Mr Steiner to install a burglar alarm in the bakery kitchen, so Maddie was able to sneak in unnoticed.

Maddie switched on the overhead light. Taking off her wellies and leaving them on the mat, she scurried across to the large pantry where Mr Steiner stored his goods on tall stacking racks. She knew the bottom five trays of the left hand rack held the 'bad' baking. These she stuffed into two bin-liners she'd brought with her – ten stollen, two dozen spritz cookies, and gingerbread shapes. There would have been more if Mr Steiner hadn't admitted to ruining quite a few because he'd been so miserable. She'd bet he'd cried a lot into the mixtures.

Maddie quietly closed the pantry door and hauled the bin bags to the mat. Feet back in her wellies, she switched off the light, dumped the bin liners in the alley, and re-locked the back door.

Triumph swept through her. That was so easy. Perhaps she was born to be a thief!

Maddie pocketed the torch – she could see the light of the snowy street at the end of the alley – and grabbed a bin liner in each hand.

Her plan was to dump them in a bin a few doors along the street so that when the bin men came in the morning all evidence of the stolen goods would be destroyed in the great grinding jaws of the bin lorry and carried away.

Emerging into the dull illumination of the streetlights, Maddie began to hurry along the pavement. The snow slowed her down but she wanted to finish the job and be back, safe in her bed, as soon as she could. In her haste she slid on some ice and went down heavily on her bum.

"Oof," she gasped.

One of the bags spilled a stollen onto the snow. Maddie, reaching for it, caught a movement on the other side of the street and froze. She peered into the gloom. From the deep shadow cast by Mr Patel's newsagent shop someone – or something – was watching her.

Fear, as cold as the snow she was sitting on, pierced Maddie's heart. It raced through her veins.

Krampus, Maddie trembled. Krampus.

The figure shifted, slightly. It was as tall as a man and burly. It began to step out of the shadows towards her. Maddie got the briefest glimpse of horns, then scrambled to her feet and ran, skidding, for home, only a few metres away. She left the bin bags behind, focussed only on one thing: getting inside before the Krampus could grab her.

She felt it behind her, felt its foul breath on her neck, even through her scarf. Maddie thought her heart was going to burst from terror.

Crying, she fumbled for her keys, almost dropped them, jammed the wrong one in the lock, and finally managed the right one. She heard a crash and a roar and then she was inside, slamming the door shut and streaking up the stairs.

Her mother and Nanny Dot came running to see what the commotion was about.

"Maddie!" Her mother and grandmother stared at her.

"Where on earth have you been?" Mum demanded, taking in Maddie's coat and wellies.

The sudden realisation of where she had been and what she had been doing doused Maddie's panic like a bucket of water on a fire. Mum would go berserk if she knew.

"I went to put the bin out," she panted. "I thought you'd forgotten and the bin men come tomorrow."

"In the middle of the night?" Mum protested.

"They come very early," Maddie squeaked.

Mum shook her head wonderingly. "I think Mr Steiner's story got you over-excited." She eyed Maddie sternly. "Now get back to bed and we'll talk about this in the morning."

"Yes, Mum," Maddie said weakly. Head hung, she shuffled past Mum and Nanny Dot (who gave her a suspicious look) and fled to her bedroom.

She only half slept for the rest of the night. Hidden deep beneath her covers Maddie had one ear tuned to the door and one tuned to the bedroom window, listening for the Krampus to come calling.

After all, she had been bad. Mr Steiner said the Krampus always knew. Maddie believed him.

#

Mr Steiner woke in the night. The roar of a car engine had startled him out of sleep. He listened to the crunch of the tyres on snow.

Lieber Gott! Who was driving through thick snow at this hour? Only a fool or someone up to no good, he thought.

Grumbling, he clambered out of his warm bed. Like Maddie's, two doors down, Mr Steiner's bedroom overlooked the street.

All was quiet out there. The bins awaiting collection in the morning stood like sentries guarding the shops and houses.

Mr Steiner spotted two bins bags dumped carelessly in the street and tutted. With all those bins who would be so lazy as to just leave them. Foxes and rats would likely tear them apart if they had any food in.

Oh well, he would be up very early in the morning and could pick them up then. Otherwise the street seemed to be fine. Whoever had been in the car was long gone. Perhaps they had been visiting friends further along the road? Christmas parties could go on late.

Satisfied that all was well Mr Steiner returned to bed, climbing back between the warm covers.

Usually if he woke in the night – which was often – he hated the empty space on Betty's side and he would go into the lounge and sleep, rather uncomfortably, on the sofa. Tonight he was exhausted from his long day of baking, and, he had to admit, a little happier after his meal with the Larkins.

Tonight, Mr Steiner went straight back to sleep.

Outside, a fox trotted out of an alleyway, drawn to the delicious smells coming from the bin bags in the road. Another followed. They nosed the bags, then tore into them with claws and teeth, snapping at gingerbread, swallowing cookies before finally each taking a stollen in their jaws and trotting off, pleased with their bounty.

Sometime later a rat arrived and made the most of the unexpected meal, carrying back as much as she could for her babies. Even a robin flew down to peck the crumbs splayed over the snow for robins sometimes sing in the depth of winter nights. At four a.m. Mr Patel's cat, Oswald, found the feast. He was unusual for a cat as he had a sweet tooth and was delighted by his good luck.

Mr Steiner's alarm woke him again at five in the morning. He still had more baking to do before the shop opened at nine.

After porridge and a cup of tea, Mr Steiner went downstairs to the bakery, fired up the ovens, switched off the alarm for the shop, and made bread.

Later he remembered the bin bags left in the street and decided to pop out and throw them in his bin. The bin collectors sometimes got funny about bags left by the bins and refused to take them.

As soon as Mr Steiner stepped out of the kitchen door the outside light sprang on. At six-forty-five on a December morning it was still as black as night, so he was glad of it. He noticed boot prints in the snow leading to and from his door. They were small so he concluded they must be Maddie's from yesterday. The sight of them made him smile. He followed them to the street and sure enough they turned in the direction of the flower shop, yet they didn't stop there. Under the streetlights he could see her small footsteps carrying on past her home, flanked by trails in the snow as though she had been dragging a sack in each hand.

Bin bags.

Mr Steiner realised that her welly prints led right to the bags that had been dumped in the street, except they were no longer where they had been. Instead they'd been torn to pieces and strewn along the road, contents scattered around in the snow.

Frowning, Mr Steiner reached the scraps. Paw prints, large and small, tracked around the bags, even the three-toed twig prints of a small bird.

A half-gnawed stollen lay on the frozen ground.

"What the…" Mr Steiner exclaimed. Who would throw away his stollen? He recognised crumbs of gingerbread too, and there! Further along he saw the sugar sprinkles on a cookie he had baked.

Slowly, Mr Steiner turned in a circle, surveying the street. Here, he saw a disturbance in the snow where someone had fallen – Maddie, because her footsteps led right up to it. He noticed at how widely spaced her prints became as though she'd run for home after dumping the bin bags. Over on the other side of the road larger footprints emerged from the shadows by Mr Patel's newsagents, trailing all down the street until they were replaced by the fresh tyre tracks of a car heading out of town - probably the one that had woken him last night.

Here was a mystery, Mr Steiner thought, shaking his head. His precious baking wasted on the ground or in the stomachs of vermin.

A worrying thought hit him. Was all his baking gone? He hurried back to his kitchen and into the pantry.

Seeing the trays of baked goodies lined up on their racks Mr Steiner heaved a great sigh of relief, until he noticed the bottom five trays were empty.

"Oh, nein," he moaned. "No, no."

Then he saw that the key was missing from its hook and he groaned.

"Madeleine," he whispered. "I thought you such a nice girl. Why have you stolen from me?"

7

"Whatever possessed you to go out in the middle of the night?" Maddie's mum repeated.

"I told you," Maddie replied around a mouthful of cornflakes. "To put the bin out."

"It was already out," Mum said. "I never forget. You could have been snatched, out on your own at that time of night."

Maddie gulped her milk. She had nearly been snatched by the Krampus but Mum would never believe that.

Nanny Dot watched her over the rim of her coffee mug. Maddie was relieved when she said: "I'm going to help Hans in the shop this morning, love. Is it all right if I take Maddie with me? Can you manage?"

Mum sighed. "I suppose he needs your help more than me. I've got Sally."

"We'll only be two doors away if you need us," Nanny said.

Mum nodded. She glanced towards the kitchen window. "Goodness!" she exclaimed. "There's a robin sitting on the window sill."

Maddie jumped to her feet.

"Keep still," Mum said. "You'll frighten it away."

Maddie approached the window very slowly. The robin looked back at her but with none of the sparky cockiness robins usually showed.

"It looks a bit depressed," Nanny Dot said. "Maybe it's ill."

Even with them all peering at it the robin didn't move, just sat, puffed out on the ledge looking glum.

"Poor thing," Mum said. "Hopefully it's just conserving energy. It'll fly away soon."

The robin was still there after Maddie had dried the breakfast dishes.

"That's so odd," Mum said. "I've never seen one stay still so long."

"I hope it'll be okay," Maddie said.

Mum nodded.

Nanny Dot and Maddie left Mum at the flower shop and carried on to the bakery. The bin men had been and Maddie was relieved to see the bin bags she had dropped were gone. A small flock of pigeons had found something to peck at in the road. The gritter came rumbling along, scattering them as it sprayed salt behind it. When it had gone past and the pigeons returned Maddie got a look at their breakfast. It was half a squashed stollen cake.

She hoped no one else recognised it, especially Mr Steiner.

Mr Steiner was waiting for them in the kitchen but yesterday's smile had disappeared. The kitchen smelled wonderfully of freshly baked bread.

"Good morning, Hans," Nanny Dot said. "Here we are as promised."

Mr Steiner nodded but he still didn't smile. Instead he looked sadly at Maddie and said: "Madeleine, have you something to give me?" He held out his hand expectantly. Maddie stared at it.

"I d…d… don't understand, Mr Steiner," she said, avoiding his gaze.

"Are you sure?" Mr Steiner asked. "I believe you have taken something of mine from the pantry."

Maddie trembled. Nanny Dot wrapped a protective arm around her. "Explain yourself, Hans. Are you accusing Maddie of something?" she demanded.

Mr Steiner crouched down and forced Maddie to look at him. "Madeleine?"

With a sob, Maddie thrust her hand into her pocket and took out Mr Steiner's spare key and handed it over.

"Madeleine!" Nanny Dot exclaimed. "Wherever did you get that?"

Mr Steiner slowly straightened. "From my pantry," he said. "Along with five trays of my baking. I found the remains of it torn out of bin bags in the street. I'm afraid Maddie's footprints gave her away as the thief."

"Thief!" Nanny Dot cried. "That's a bit strong. I'm sure there's a good explanation. Isn't there, Maddie?"

Maddie burst out: "Yes there is, Nanny. Truly there is. But I didn't want Mr Steiner to know about it."

"Know about what?" Mr Steiner looked bewildered.

"It's your baking, Mr Steiner. It's magic!"

"Magic! What nonsense is this, child? You must tell me the truth. Why did you steal my baking?"

"Ohhhh," Nanny groaned. "Oh, Maddie. So this is where you went last night."

"Yes," Maddie confessed. "I was going to put the key back this morning before Mr Steiner noticed. But I had to do it, Nanny. I couldn't let people buy Mr Steiner's bad stuff."

"I beg your pardon," Mr Steiner said, offended. "I don't sell any 'bad stuff.'"

"Oh, it doesn't taste bad, Mr Steiner," Maddie said. "It just makes them feel bad."

Mr Steiner began to splutter indignantly but Nanny stepped in swiftly.

"Let's sit down and I'll explain properly before it's time to open the shop," Nanny said, guiding Mr Steiner to the workbench. "Come sit here, Maddie," she said, patting the stool next to her.

Nanny Dot began. "Hans, Maddie believes that whatever emotion you are feeling goes into your baking…"

"You believe it too, Nanny Dot," Maddie interrupted.

Nanny blushed. "Yes, well… so. Anyway, she noticed…"

"So did you!"

Nanny glared at her and began again. "Maddie noticed first, and I came to agree with her: your grief over Betty has affected your baking."

"I saw you crying into your mixture, Mr Steiner," Maddie said sadly.

Mr Steiner looked mortified. "You spied on me?"

"No! I came to deliver your card," Maddie protested. "I…"

Nanny Dot gave her a look that shut her up. "We noticed that eating your stollen put me and Lily in a terrible mood. Sad, weepy and irritable."

"Many people are like that at Christmas," Mr Steiner said.

"True," Nanny agreed. "But not children. Maddie and two of her friends were in a right state after eating your *sachertorte*."

"Sugar crash," Mr Steiner dismissed her.

Maddie, frustrated, took up the story. "Grownups always say things like that. But I took a scientific approach, Mr Steiner. I decided to test my theory using your stollen."

She told him about her experiment on George Wilkins in the park.

"Coincidence," said Mr Steiner, although by now he was smiling.

"Ooooh," Maddie cried, beating her fists on the wooden table in frustration. "It's not. When I told Nanny Dot we decided to cheer you up. Then Mum ate your gingerbread and it made her really happy, so there, you see, it's true. Your baking is magic. *You* are magic Mr Steiner!"

Mr Steiner shook his head in disbelief but his smile was wider. "So," he said after a moment. "I still don't understand why you broke into my kitchen and stole my goods."

Maddie almost rolled her eyes at his stupidity. Hadn't she just told him? "Because you baked the things on the bottom five trays the day before yesterday," she told him. "When you were really, really sad. I couldn't let people buy them, Mr Steiner. They'd be sad at Christmas time. And I didn't want to tell you because you'd feel awful about it."

Suddenly Maddie felt like crying. Her lower lip trembled and a tear rolled down her cheek. "I thought you wouldn't believe me," she sobbed. "And now you don't."

"*Nein*, *nein*, *nein*," Mr Steiner said, rising from his stool to go to her. He pulled a large clean handkerchief out of his pocket and dabbed at her eyes with it. Tenderly he made her blow her nose on it and handed it to Nanny Dot who grimaced and took the handkerchief reluctantly between her finger and thumb.

"Madeleine Larkin," Mr Steiner said. "If this is what you think then this is what it is. You are the sweetest little girl I have ever known, *ja*?"

Maddie sniffed.

"You're certainly the silliest," Nanny laughed fondly. "I wish you'd just told me. I could have come up with a solution that didn't involve burglary."

#

Maddie felt so relieved after her confession that she managed to forget about the Krampus until late afternoon when the sun began to sink and the night to creep in.

Business in the bakery was brisk; the delicious goodies flew off the shelves as Mr Steiner rang up the cash till while Nanny Dot and Maddie put the orders together.

Because of Maddie's theft, Mr Steiner ran out of his famous stollen very quickly. Customers who'd come in specifically for their Christmas stollen grumbled, especially those from out of town; they'd driven through the snow to get here.

Mr Steiner wrote out a sign. He winked at Maddie as he put it up. It said: 'Due to an oven failure we have run out of stollen. However if you leave your order with us we will have it ready for tomorrow. Thank you and Merry Christmas.'

The grumpiest woman in town, Margaret Tolliver, began loudly complaining to everyone around her as she waited in the queue.

"Nearly broke my neck getting here," she moaned. "And for nothing. No way to run a business this. I've been coming here for fifteen years and I've never been turned away without my Christmas stollen. I've a good mind to take my business elsewhere."

Maddie grabbed a tray of cookies and marched out from around the counter. As she reached Mrs Tolliver, Maddie heard her say to her neighbour: "He's let things slide since his wife died."

Maddie almost snatched the cookies back but forced herself to smile sweetly and said: "Have a sugar cookie, Mrs Tolliver. They're really nice."

Mrs Tolliver peered at her over the glasses she wore perched on the end of her nose and wrinkled her nose as though she was going to refuse while at the same time her bony hand whipped out and snatched a star-shaped cookie.

"I suppose this will stick to my dentures," she sniffed, taking a bite.

Maddie passed along the queue offering the cookies until the tray was empty. People munched as they waited.

Soon the grumbles changed to a happy hum as folks began to chat and laugh. Even Mrs Tolliver smiled. "Never mind," she said, as she was served by Nanny Dot, who packed her bread and gingerbread and took her order for stollen. "I suppose this means it'll just be all the fresher for Christmas."

"Look, Mr Steiner," Maddie whispered. "I told you your baking was magic. The cookies we baked yesterday have made everyone happy."

"That's because you gave them away for free," Mr Steiner replied, but his eyes twinkled.

Maddie had a sudden thought. Excitedly she turned to Nanny. "I know what's wrong with that robin, Nanny. Can I nip home for a minute?"

Nanny Dot was too busy to protest.

"I won't be long," Maddie said to Mr Steiner. She carried the empty cookie tray through the passageway that connected the shop to the kitchen and found a little polythene bag to empty the crumbs into.

Slipping on her coat and wellingtons, Maddie scurried home, waving to her mum as she passed the flower shop.

The robin still huddled miserably on the windowsill. It didn't even seem to notice she was there.

Very slowly, Maddie opened the window. Fortunately it slid upwards so she wasn't in danger of knocking the robin off its ledge. She expected it to fly away – that's what any self-respecting robin should have done – but it merely flapped its wings half-heartedly and watched her with its dull black eye.

"You ate the stollen I dropped, didn't you?" Maddie crooned soothingly. "And now you feel too sad to fly. Well, eat some of these," she said, dropping the crumbs on the sill. "I think you'll feel better."

Maddie backed away from the window but the robin didn't move. She decided to leave it alone for a moment and went to the fridge to get a glass of milk and an apple from the fruit bowl. As she sat down at the kitchen table she caught a movement out of the corner of her eye. The robin was pecking at the crumbs.

Pleased, Maddie ate her apple and drank her milk.

Ten minutes later Maddie cautiously approached the window.

The robin cocked his head. His eye sparkled as he puffed his red breast proudly. He seemed to give her a little bow and then he was off with a beat of his wings, away into the blue sky.

Maddie clapped her hands in delight.

#

Mr Steiner turned the bakery door sign to 'closed' with a sigh of relief. "Thank goodness," he said. Below the closed sign the opening and closing times printed on the door read:

Monday closed.

8.00 am to 2.00pm Tues to Thursday

8.30 am to 4.30 pm Friday to Saturday.

Sunday closed.

Today was Tuesday and they were all very grateful for the early closing.

Maddie had grabbed a sandwich with Mum at twelve. Nanny Dot took her lunch break at twelve thirty but Mr Steiner had worked through the entire morning with only a break for coffee.

"No wonder you're so thin," Nanny Dot chided him. "Eat and have a rest before you start again."

Mr Steiner cut himself a thick slice of pumpernickel bread, produced some ham and butter from the industrial size fridge, and sat down to eat.

Nanny Dot shook her head. "And where is the salad?" Nanny believed in eating your greens.

Mr Steiner rolled his eyes and winked at Maddie. "I am German," he announced. "I have the constitution of a horse."

Nanny Dot snorted as Maddie giggled. "Horses eat grass," Nanny pointed out. "They live on salad."

"What's constitution?" Maddie asked.

"He means he's strong and healthy," Nanny Dot explained.

Maddie looked at Mr Steiner. With his silver hair and round glasses he didn't look strong and healthy, but then neither did Sophie Tong, who was the smallest, skinniest kid in class, but she could run faster than anyone and always won on sports day. "I think you must be strong, Mr Steiner, to do all your baking. All you seem to do is work."

"*Ja*," Mr Steiner agreed. "It is harder without Betty to help. She did such a lot for me." He bent and pulled up his trouser legs. "Look," he pointed. "Odd socks. My Betty would never have let me wear odd socks, but I keep forgetting to do the washing. Betty did it all for me." His eyes misted over.

Maddie panicked. "Don't be sad, Mr Steiner. You have to bake soon."

Nanny put a hand on her shoulder. "It's all right to be sad sometimes, Maddie. It can feel good to share that with your friends, can't it Hans?"

Mr Steiner blinked away his tears and his smile broke through like the sun. "It is very good," he said. "*Und* so nice to be able to talk about Betty again."

The afternoon was such a lot of fun. They played Christmas music as they worked and sang along.

Mr Steiner had whipped up various cookie mixes the previous evening, storing them in the fridge in clingfilm, so that all Maddie had to do was get them out and feed them through the cookie press, changing the cutters to produce different shapes. Soon they had dozens of cookies and gingerbreads baking in the ovens. Nanny Dot was in charge of taking them in and out and putting them on the cooling racks and then sliding them on to the stackable towers.

Mr Steiner totted up the orders for stollen they'd taken and then added on extra for new customers.

For the first time in over a year the bakery was alive with music and laughter. It was a glory of flour and sugar and marzipan and icing and spice. Yellow butter gleamed; brown sugar and cinnamon glistened over apple strudel waiting to be baked; yeast worked its age-old magic on dough.

And Mr Steiner talked. He told them about learning to bake with his father in Bavaria. He told them he'd met Betty when she was only seventeen while her army father was posted in Germany, and how they had ridden around on a motorbike and sidecar, Betty bravely hanging on for dear life in the sidecar as they took the corners. One day Mr Steiner took a corner but the sidecar didn't, poor Betty spinning off in another direction entirely until the sidecar ran into a ditch. He'd zoomed over, terrified she'd been hurt, or worse, only to find her covered in mud laughing hysterically. When he tried to pull her out she pulled him down into the mud with her. They'd laughed so much they could hardly climb out. Sneaking her back on to her father's army base without being seen had been quite an achievement.

Nanny knew exactly what a sidecar was and had ridden in one herself before she was married.

"What is a sidecar?" Maddie asked.

"It's what Gromit rides in with Wallace," Nanny said. "I used to ride in one myself before I was married. You never really see them now. Health and safety I suppose. Mind you, they were death traps."

"Really?"

"Well, potentially," Nanny Dot said. "It wasn't very nice to ride in the sidecar. You were sitting in a tin box on the ground with wheels and whenever you stopped behind a car at a traffic light you got all the exhaust in your face."

"Sounds horrible," Maddie said.

Nanny and Mr Steiner agreed, although by the dreamy look on their faces they didn't mean it.

"Did you ride in it with Granddad?" Maddie asked.

Nanny Dot's expression became even dreamier. "No," she said. "I used to go on it to band practice and gigs." She lost the dreamy look and glanced at Maddie. "Actually I used to ride with Phil Turner – you know, you met him in the café yesterday."

Maddie's interest quickened. "Was he your boyfriend?"

Nanny Dot smiled secretively. "I stepped out with him once or twice. Nothing serious."

Maddie made exaggerated smooching noises. "Did you kiss him?"

Nanny Dot guffawed, swatting at her. "That's none of your business, cheeky."

"Was this before you met Granddad?"

Nanny looked outraged. "Of course it was."

"Why did you stop playing the trumpet?" Mr Steiner asked.

Nanny Dot's expression sharpened. "My husband didn't like it. Funny really. He liked it well-enough before we married. In fact he first saw me playing in a club. It's what attracted him. After that…" She trailed off.

Mr Steiner shrugged. "Well I think both Maddie and I would like to hear you play it. *Ja*, Maddie?"

"*Ja*!" Maddie said, perfectly mimicking Mr Steiner's accent and making them all laugh.

It was almost four when Mr Steiner realised he'd forgotten to cash up and take the day's takings to the post office next door. He was still elbow deep in stollen dough so Nanny Dot offered to do it for him.

"I do it for the flower shop all the time," she said. "So I don't mind, as long as you trust me."

Mr Steiner gave a curt bow and said of course he trusted the grandmother of Madeleine Larkin, to which Nanny Dot gave him a wry smile, saying. "She did burgle you last night."

"Nanny!" Maddie threatened to fling icing at her. Nanny ducked out of the door, laughing.

After she'd gone Maddie realised how dark it was getting outside and remembered the Krampus. Fear crept in. What if he came back tonight? Perhaps it didn't matter that she'd confessed. She'd still committed the crime.

She bungled icing a couple of spritz cookies and kept glancing at the gathering shadows outside.

"Are you all right, Maddie?" Mr Steiner asked. "You must be tired. Perhaps it is time you went home."

"I'm all right," Maddie lied.

She tried to put the Krampus out of her mind and concentrate on her task but she only ruined another cookie.

A nasty thought slithered into her mind. What if it had been the Krampus who stole her father? What if he came with the snow? Had her dad done something bad?

It was the sort of anxious thought that started small, then wormed its way into your brain and fed on your fear until it was fat and sleek as a leech and it was all you could think of.

Maddie jumped as Mr Steiner gently took her icing-bag away.

"What's wrong, Maddie? You look so pale."

Maddie looked into his kind eyes. "I saw the Krampus last night," she whispered.

Mr Steiner blinked. This time it was he who looked worried. "Oh *mein liebling*. I should never have told you that story. It has frightened you. The Krampus is not real, Maddie."

"You saw him."

"It was my father."

Maddie shook her head emphatically. "You don't know that for sure."

Mr Steiner sighed. "Anyway," he said brightening. "The Krampus only comes out on the fifth of December, so you couldn't have seen him."

"In Germany," Maddie said. "He might come later here."

"The Krampus is make-believe, Maddie," Mr Steiner insisted.

"I saw him," Maddie said, equally insistent. "Last night, after I'd stolen your baking. He was watching me. I saw him in the shadows by Mr Patel's. He had horns,

Mr Steiner, just like you said. Then he started to come towards me and I ran for home as fast as I could. He nearly got me too, but Mum and Nanny Dot woke up so he couldn't come in." She finished breathlessly.

Mr Steiner frowned. "Is that why you left the bags in the middle of the street? I wondered why you didn't put them in a bin."

"I was going to," Maddie said. "But I forgot about them when I saw the Krampus. I'm scared he'll come back tonight. He knows I burgled you, Mr Steiner, and I didn't put the stuff back the way you put your brothers' toys back."

Mr Steiner said nothing for a moment. He appeared to be deep in thought. "I tell you what," he finally said. "Now, I don't think you really saw the Krampus, Maddie…" He held out his hand to stop her protest. "But just in case I'm wrong I'll tell you what I'm going to do."

"What?"

"The Krampus will only come once he thinks the grown-ups are asleep. I am going to have a nap this evening and set my alarm to wake me up. Then I'm going to sit by the window and watch for the Krampus.

Of course he won't come, but if he does, I will see him and go out and tell him what a good girl you are and why you stole my baking."

"Would he listen to you?"

"Of course he would. If he really does exist then he will remember me from my childhood. He gave me a second chance, remember, *und* my naughty brothers."

"Will you really do that for me?" Maddie asked.

"I will."

"You'll keep guard all night?"

"*Ja.*"

"You won't fall asleep?"

"I am often awake all night, Maddie. Sometimes I find it hard to sleep."

"Thank you, Mr Steiner," Maddie cried, relief almost exploding out of her. "Thank you so much."

8

Mr Steiner had every intention of keeping his word to Maddie even though he didn't believe in the Krampus.

The Krampus was a *wunder marchen* – a fairy tale – for children. Yet the small boy he'd once been shuddered at the memory of his encounter with it and still secretly believed it hadn't been his papa.

What bothered Mr Steiner the most was Maddie's idea that the Krampus had taken her father.

He realised how much Maddie missed having a dad.

Whatever had happened to Vince Larkin? Once again he felt ashamed of how little interest he'd taken when the young man disappeared. How wrapped up he'd been in his own contained life, Mr Steiner thought.

All he'd ever wanted was Betty and his bakery. He had his friends from his Oompah band and even then he wasn't inclined to socialise with them outside band practice and the occasional concert.

He'd only joined in the search for Vince at Betty's insistence.

He'd refused to give much thought to the young woman who, only two doors down, was pacing the floorboards with her month-old baby, waiting for a husband who would never return.

How would he have felt if Betty stepped out one night and disappeared? Poof! Like magic. Just gone, leaving no trace.

That December had brought the kind of weather he'd endured as a boy in the foothills of the Alps. The evening Vince Larkin had supposedly popped along to the Co-op for nappies the snow fell so heavily it obliterated all evidence – tyre tracks, footprints – within minutes of their appearance. By the time Lily Larkin raised the alarm any sign of Vince's passage was gone, stolen by the snow.

And how much care and attention had Mr Steiner given to his neighbour, Maddie Larkin, growing up without her daddy?

Not much. He'd left Betty to do the caring for people. Her heart was big enough, he'd thought, to give to everyone. In the end, it was her heart that had worn out and broken down. Perhaps if he'd cared for others a little more, he could have shared some of the burden on her heart and she'd be here now.

"Ah," Mr Steiner said, jumping up. "*Aufhören, selbstmitleid.* Stop feeling sorry for myself. I must do something to help Maddie and her family."

It was seven in the evening. Mr Steiner went into his study, where he did all his accounts for the bakery, and turned on his computer.

He typed 'Vincent Larkin' into Google. The search came up with all sorts of profiles but none matched the Vince Larkin Mr Steiner vaguely remembered, either in age or looks. Next he brought up the U.K. Bureau for Missing Persons. There was nothing on that but sadness. So many missing people but not a trace of Vince.

Disheartened, Mr Steiner went into the small kitchen of his flat to make a coffee. Unusually, he fancied something sweet, so went downstairs to raid the bakery pantry, returning with a fat slice of apple cake.

It had been a long time since he had eaten his own *apfelkuchen.*

Ah! He closed his eyes in bliss. Tasting it took him back to his papa's orchard, gathering apples for the cake. How Betty had loved this recipe.

Renewed hope surged through him. He would not give up. He would find Maddie's father for her or at least find out what happened to him.

Mr Steiner went to the sideboard and took a pretty floral-patterned book out of a drawer. This was the address book where Betty had neatly recorded the contacts for their friends and family.

Mr Steiner flicked to the 'T' section, trailing his finger down until he found Turner. Philip Turner.

Philip played the trombone in the Oompah band. A retired police officer, he could be a bit pompous but was always ready to help.

Mr Steiner picked up the phone and hesitated. He'd not officially dropped out of the Oompah band, simply stopped turning up for practice. He hadn't meant to be rude; he just stopped wanting to see other people after Betty died. Whenever one of his friends called he made an excuse why he couldn't join them. Eventually they stopped calling.

This was for Maddie, he told himself, and punched in the numbers.

Phil answered on the fourth ring.

"Hello Phil. It's Hans."

There was the briefest pause on the other end before: "Hans! Great to hear from you. Did you get my card?"

"*Ja.* Thank you. Maddie Larkin gave it to me."

"Dorothy Flowers granddaughter? Yes. I bumped into them in the café."

"Yes, they said. Er, Phil it's actually Maddie I want to ask about, or rather about her father, Vince Larkin. He went missing. Do you remember?"

"I do," Phil said. "I was the sergeant on the desk the night they reported him gone. Terrible blizzard that night, I remember."

"He went to the Co-op to buy some nappies."

"That was the story," Phil said.

"Story? What do you mean?"

Phil gave a bark of a laugh. "I mean that's what he told his wife. But I think he had no intention of coming back. I think he found himself tied down too young with a wife and baby and wanted out."

"You can't be sure," Mr Steiner said.

"No one was sure. He certainly made it look like he was coming back – didn't take his phone or pack any clothes, but he might have had it all planned in advance. Had a lift waiting for him – maybe a fancy woman. Who knows?"

Mr Steiner frowned. "I don't want to believe that. Maybe something happened to him. Perhaps he had an accident?"

"There was no evidence of one – mind you it was snowing so hard it was impossible to tell. But even if he had and someone had taken him to hospital why didn't he come back? We notified local doctors' surgeries and hospitals. No one reported anything." Phil hesitated. "Why do you want to know about it now? It was ten years ago."

Mr Steiner sighed. "Madeleine is such a sweet girl," he said. "Her family have been so kind to me recently.

If I could find out what happened to her father – maybe even find him – it would be something I could give to her."

"Dangerous," Phil warned. "If he abandoned her and didn't want to be found that would hurt her very much."

"I know," Mr Steiner said. "In that case I probably wouldn't tell her."

"Tell you what," Phil said. "After Christmas, if you still want to try to find him, I'll help you. I still have contacts on the force."

"Would you?" Mr Steiner brightened. "That would be *wunderbar*."

"Yep. But only if you do something for me," Phil added.

"Oh?"

"Play the accordion at a Christmas concert we're doing at a homeless shelter on Christmas Eve afternoon. Our accordion player's gone down with flu. Besides he's not a patch on you."

Mr Steiner thought about it. He hadn't played his accordion since his Bettina died. Still, if Phil would help him find Maddie's dad he should return a favour.

"All right," he said. "But I am very rusty."

"Fantastic. And one other thing…"

"What's that?" Mr Steiner asked.

"Can you ask Dorothy Flowers to come along? She can bring her trumpet."

"Oh *ja*?" Mr Steiner laughed. "Any other reason you want her to come?"

"Damn right there is," Phil said. "She's still the best looking woman I know."

"What will your wife say to that?"

"She left me for a tuba player in June," Phil said.

"I'm sorry."

"Don't be," Phil said. "Best thing that's ever happened to me. Just make sure you ask Dorothy."

Mr Steiner smiled. "I will ask her," he said. "But I don't know if she will come."

"Good enough. I'll pick you up at two on Friday. You'll have shut the shop by then?"

"*Ja*. We'll close at lunchtime on Christmas Eve."

"Excellent. See you then. And Hans…"

"*Ja*?"

"It's good to hear your voice again."

They said goodbye and hung up.

Mr Steiner was glad he'd rung Phil. Feeling warm inside, he retrieved his accordion case from the study and undid the clasps.

Inside lay a beautiful old piano accordion. Mr Steiner admired the gleam of its walnut wood and worn keys. Lovingly he lifted it out of the case, placed the strap over his shoulder, and squeezed the bellows.

"*Hallo*, *alter freund*," he murmured. Hello, old friend.

It was hard work squeezing the sound out. His accordion muscles were stiff from lack of use. He would need some practise before Christmas Eve if he was going to play with the Oompah band.

At nine o' clock he needed a rest. Curling up on his sofa, Mr Steiner pulled one of Betty's crocheted throws over himself and fell asleep. He didn't mean to sleep so long, and woke to find the logs in his wood-burning stove had reduced to embers. He heard the church clock strike twelve times. Midnight.

He was supposed to be on watch for Maddie.

Turning off the lamps, he opened the curtains and dragged a chair over to the window, positioning himself so he could see the street and the deep shadows of Mr

Patel's newsagents. As he watched he gently worked the accordion, making it wheeze out a soft tune.

The pavements were still patchy with snow, although the grit and traffic of the day had cleared most of it.

He hoped that Maddie was sleeping soundly, free from her fear of the Krampus.

A couple stumbled along the street, giggling, no doubt full of Christmas spirit from the pub or a party. Mr Steiner watched their progress wistfully, recalling the days of his youth with Betty. His tune turned sad as he remembered.

Abruptly he stopped playing and leaned forward. There, in the shadows, had he seen a movement?

Probably Mr Patel's cat, or a fox, Mr Steiner told himself. Certainly not the Krampus for he didn't exist.

He peered into the darkness and gradually, as his eyes adjusted, he made out a black man-sized shape lurking in the setback doorway of Mr Patel's shop.

"*Mein Gott*!" Mr Steiner exclaimed.

As he watched the figure moved forward slightly. Mr Steiner made out the silhouette of horns on its head which was tilted up at Maddie's window.

“*Sapperlot*!” Mr Steiner said, wrenching the accordion off as he leapt to his feet. He hurried to the flat door where his boots stood, yanked them on, and, without taking the time to pull on a coat, ran downstairs, unlocked the outside door, and scurried down the alleyway towards the street.

He must have made some noise because the figure was already moving, turning to run.

“Wait,” Mr Steiner called, waving. His heart pounded. Whether this was the Krampus or a man, Mr Steiner wanted to know what he was doing watching Maddie’s window.

The figure broke into a sprint down the middle of the road. Out of the cover of the shadows Mr Steiner saw that it was a man.

“Stop,” he called, but the man kept on running.

Mr Steiner gave chase, forgetting his age and the slippery conditions. Luckily, he wasn’t the one who slipped over; the man fell with a cry and lost his horns. He was on his feet in a second and running again until he reached a car.

Mr Steiner reached the place where the man had fallen. On the road, was the oddest hat Mr Steiner had ever seen. It was a sturdy knitted beany yet sprouting from it –also knitted - was a pair of horns. These did not spiral like a ram's (or a Krampus's) but curved upwards the way horns did on Viking helmets.

Mr Steiner grabbed it, waving it. "Wait, your hat," he said, running towards the car.

The rear lights came on as the engine roared into life and the driver peeled away from the kerb and accelerated away, leaving Mr Steiner panting in the street, holding the peculiar hat.

Slowly, he made his way back, glancing up at Maddie's window to make sure she hadn't seen the goings on.

To his relief her curtain remained firmly closed.

Back in the warmth of his flat, Mr Steiner felt shaky. Goodness, what possessed him to go chasing after a man in the middle of the night?

And it had been a man, he chastised himself. Not an imaginary Krampus. Tsk!

He sank on to the sofa, looking at the hat in his hand. It was a knitted helmet, he realised; a joke hat but a warm one that would keep you cosy on a freezing night.

Why had the man been watching Maddie's flat? It was creepy. He was the 'Krampus' Maddie had seen, no doubt. No wonder she was terrified, poor *liebling*.

Mr Steiner went to the kitchen to make a cup of tea. Stirring milk into it he pondered the situation.

Should he tell Mrs Larkin about the man? Or the police? Was Maddie in danger?

Slowly, another thought formed; rather a wonderful one.

What if the man watching Maddie's window wasn't a stranger? What if *he* was her father?

The idea excited Mr Steiner. Perhaps Vincent Larkin was working up the courage to return.

9

Maddie woke up full of energy. She'd slept the night through, despite her fears, feeling safe because she trusted Mr Steiner to look out for her.

"Morning, Mum," she sang, bouncing into the kitchen.

Mum smiled at her over her bowl of porridge. "Somebody's in a chipper mood."

"Only two sleeps now till Christmas," Maddie said.

"I know," Mum said. "Which reminds me; I know Mr Steiner needed your help but I could do with you running some errands for me and doing a bit of cleaning. I've texted Nanny and she's sure they can manage without you for the morning."

"Aw," Maddie pulled her face. She'd been looking forward to seeing Mr Steiner. "Muuuum."

"Don't 'mum' me," Mum said. "I've got a shop to run and Christmas to get ready for and no time to do it all. It may not be as much fun as the bakery but it needs doing all the same."

"Yes but…" Maddie began.

Mum cut her off with a curt wave of her hand. "No buts, Madeleine. I need you to do some jobs for me. I'm working flat out, and if you want a nice Christmas without me being too tired and grumpy to enjoy it you'll do as I say. Besides," she said, looking at Maddie's sulky expression. "I've made a decision you'll like but I'll only do it if you do your chores."

Maddie brightened. "What's that?"

"I'm going to invite Mr Steiner round for Christmas dinner."

"Yes!" Maddie ran around the table to throw her arms around Mum. "Thank you."

"And you'll help me out?"

"Yes," Maddie said. "Just tell me what to do."

"I've written a list," Mum said. "What's that?" she said suddenly, looking at the window.

Maddie turned to look. "It's the robin," she cried.

The robin cocked his head, regarding them with his sparkling eye, then tapped twice on the window, dropped something on the windowsill and flew away.

Maddie went to see what he'd left. It was a bright red holly berry.

She slid up the window and plucked it from the ledge. "He's left us a present."

"More likely he's put it there so he can eat it later," Mum said, looking flabbergasted.

Maddie knew better. The robin was paying her back for the gingerbread crumbs which had saved his life. If he'd remained depressed on the windowsill any longer he would have died of cold.

Even the robin knew that Mr Steiner's baking was magic.

#

While Maddie was working her way through Mum's extensive list of chores, Mr Steiner was busy in his shop with Nanny Dot. Business was brisk so he had no time to ponder last night's events.

He enjoyed working with Dorothy Flowers. She was quick, efficient and had a knack of making the customers laugh and smile. He saw where Maddie got her good nature from. He'd noticed that Dorothy always wore polka dots somewhere on her person. Today it was a gauzy, white-dotted red scarf tied nattily around her neck, while yesterday they'd appeared on her cardigan in a navy and deep pink combination.

When he mentioned it to her she beamed. "It's because of my nickname: 'Dot'," she explained. "Dot is short for Dorothy. I started to wear polka dots years ago. It's a bit like my signature."

At eleven Maddie popped her head in, on her way to the greengrocer's to pick up an order for Mum. Mr Steiner gave her two generous slices of *apfelkuchen* for her and Mum to have with lunch.

"I'm going to give the crumbs to my robin," she called back as she left.

By closing time at two neither he nor Nanny Dot had taken a lunch break. All the people who'd missed the stollen yesterday had turned up for their orders and the shop was packed with new and return customers.

Mr Steiner stuck another notice to the door announcing Christmas Eve closing was at midday tomorrow and the bakery would be shut until New Year.

This was standard practice for the bakery, hence the last minute rush to buy Mr Steiner's goodies.

Of course, having sold almost everything Mr Steiner would have to bake like mad again this afternoon. Ah, he shrugged inwardly. Such was life. And the truth was that he'd begun to enjoy baking the way he used to before Betty died.

He almost felt guilty for it, as though without Betty he shouldn't be able to feel pleasure. *Nein.* That was not what Betty would want. Betty would want him to be happy, *ja*?

"Do we have time for a late lunch?" Nanny Dot asked. "It would be good to get out before starting in the kitchen."

"You don't have to stay, you've done enough," Mr Steiner said. Her look stopped him. It was a 'don't start that nonsense' look.

"Let's grab a quick bite at the Blue Teapot," Nanny Dot suggested.

Mr Steiner agreed. Although he had a lot to do, a proper break would do them good. He went upstairs to fetch his coat and hat. Seeing the Viking hat on the table where he'd left it he stuffed it in his coat pocket on a whim and took it with him.

It was quiet in the Blue Teapot Café, the lunch rush was over, and only a few people lingered over coffees.

Nanny Dot ordered quiche and salad while Mr Steiner chose a beef and horseradish sandwich.

"I talked to Phil Turner yesterday," Mr Steiner told Nanny Dot.

"Oh, yes?" she said, unconsciously patting her hair.

"I've agreed to stand in for the Oompah band's accordion player tomorrow afternoon. They're playing at the homeless shelter in Great Alderton."

"He mentioned that," Nanny Dot said. "That's great, Hans. It'll be nice for you to play again."

"Well," Hans said. "Perhaps it would be nice for you too. Phil wants you to come."

"What?" Nanny Dot laughed. "I might've cleaned my trumpet but I'm far from being able to play it again."

"C'mon," Mr Steiner teased. "Don't tell me you haven't had a toot on it."

"Last night," Nanny Dot admitted. "I was terrible. I could hardly get any puff."

"Ah!" Mr Steiner said. "I know the feeling. I got out my accordion. My arms were all out of 'puff' also."

Nanny Dot chortled. "Doesn't sound like either us should go tomorrow."

"We could practise tonight," Mr Steiner suggested.

They emerged from the café to find the light was already fading, although it wasn't yet three o' clock, and Christmas lights twinkled along the street.

Mr Steiner caught a flash of cerise up ahead. It was Maddie, coming out of the Co-op with another girl. He was about to call to her when a boy, lounging against the wall of the Co-op yelled loudly. "How's it going Maddie-no-dad? Looking forward to another Christmas without your Daddy?"

"Shut up, George," the girl beside Maddie shouted back.

"You know he left you because you're so ugly," George ignored her, focussing his attention on Maddie.

Maddie stuck her hands on her hips. "You still crying over your dog, George? Everybody saw you."

The boy's face reddened. He clenched his fist and moved towards Maddie threateningly.

Mr Steiner quickened his stride to step in, Nanny Dot matching him, when a brutal looking man stepped out of the Co-op and cuffed George around the ears.

"Shut it," he growled. "I don't need no trouble from you." He grabbed his son roughly by the arm and dragged him down the street.

Mr Steiner stopped, catching Nanny Dot's arm, and let the two girls march away, heads close together in conversation.

Seeing Maddie being teased like that made Mr Steiner more determined to find her father. Pulling the Viking hat out of his pocket, he showed it to Nanny Dot and said: "I have something I must tell you."

#

"And he has terrible horns, devil hooves and fire-red eyes," Maddie told Suzy, as they sprawled on their bellies on Maddie's bed.

"That's scary," Suzy replied.

"Uhuh," said Maddie. "And he carries away bad children and eats them up."

"What's he called again? A crap man?"

"No," Maddie started giggling. "A Krampus. Not a crap man."

Suzy started giggling too and soon they were rolling around hysterically. Back under control, Suzy said. "I wish there really was a Krampus. It would carry George Wilkins away. Why does he have to be so mean?"

Maddie shuddered. There *was* a Krampus but she didn't dare admit to Suzy she'd seen it. Suzy got scared too easily.

"I don't know," she said. "He's always on about my dad but I think I'd rather have no dad than one like his."

"Yeah," Susie agreed. "He's horrible." She rolled onto her back, staring up at the stars on Maddie's ceiling. They weren't so noticeable now but in the dark, when she came for sleepovers, they shone like real stars. "I wonder what happened to your dad," she said.

They'd talked about this loads of times over the years, making up stories around his disappearance – he'd gone off to save the universe, or been kidnapped by pirates, or fell down a crack in the ground to the centre of the earth. Every story ended with him trying to find his way back home, and one day he would.

Maddie was quiet for a moment. "I wish Mum would talk about him," she sighed. "She won't even let Nanny Dot say anything."

"Why?" Suzy asked.

"Dunno. She just gets mad when I ask her. And Mum doesn't get mad about much."

"No," Suzy said. "Mostly she's nice. Like the way you can stay up till you're ready to go to bed. My mum makes me go whether I'm sleepy or not." Just then her phone rang.

Maddie watched Suzy pull the phone out of her pocket. She was envious. Mum wouldn't let her have her own phone until she was eleven and that was almost an entire year away. Both Suzy and Daisy had phones– smartphones too! And they had dads.

Suzy spoke to her mum. "I'm at Maddie's. What? Yeaaah. Okay. I'm leaving now." She pulled a face that made Maddie laugh and hung up.

"I forgot my Auntie Pam was arriving. I'm supposed to be home when she gets there. I gotta go."

Maddie walked her out. She stepped into the flower shop to see Mum.

"Has Suzy gone?" Mum asked, waving off a customer.

"Yes. Her Auntie Pam's arriving today." She and Mum exchanged grins. They'd heard all about the Auntie Pam's visits many times before. She came for a week over Christmas, and nothing Suzy's mum and dad did was good enough for her.

"Thank goodness we don't have any relatives like that," Mum said. "Did you get all your chores done?"

"Yes. But the Co-op had run out of cream."

"Never mind," Mum said. "I'm sure we'll manage. I just wanted an extra carton as Mr Steiner's coming."

"He said yes?" Maddie bobbed up and down excitedly.

"Well, no. I haven't actually asked him yet. I just assumed…"

"Can I go ask him?"

"Go on then," Mum said. "But don't be disappointed if he says no."

Mr Steiner was in his bakery kitchen whizzing together ingredients when Maddie knocked. At first he didn't hear her, so she pushed open the door and stuck her head in.

He caught sight of her, grinned, and waved her in.

"I am very behind again, Madeleine," he said. "Are you here to give a hand?"

"I will do, Mr Steiner," Maddie said. She sprang into action, first tying back her hair and washing her hands before donning the apron that reached almost to her feet. After three days of wearing it she considered it to be her apron.

"I made more dough this morning," Mr Steiner instructed. "Get it out of the fridge and you can put it through the cookie press."

Maddie was an expert at this by now and made quick work of it, handing the loaded trays to Mr Steiner so he could slide them in the oven and set the timer.

"We make a good team, *ja*?" Mr Steiner said.

"*Ja*," Maddie replied. "Very good." She climbed onto a stool. "Mr Steiner?"

"*Ja*?"

"Mum wants you to have Christmas dinner with us. She told me to ask you."

Mr Steiner looked up from his kneading. "That is very kind of her," he said carefully. "But I don't want to impose on your Christmas day. *Das ist* family time."

"I don't exactly know what 'impose' means," Maddie said, "but I don't think you'll be doing it. I want you to come, Mum does, and so will Nanny Dot. Look, here she is." Maddie pointed to the kitchen door where Nanny Dot had just appeared in her cheery red beret.

Nanny seemed startled to see her. She pushed into the kitchen, carrying a large bag.

"Hello," she said. "Have you finished all your jobs?"

Maddie rolled her eyes. "Ages ago," she said. "Nanny, Mum's invited Mr Steiner for Christmas dinner. Don't you think that's an awesome idea?"

"Awesome," Nanny repeated wryly, winking at Mr Steiner. "I think it's wonderful. You've said yes, I hope?"

Mr Steiner held up his floury hands in defeat. "I can see 'no' won't do."

"*Nein*," Maddie said, clapping her hands. "Oh, it'll be so nice to have four of us, won't it Nanny Dot?"

Maddie, Nanny Dot, and Mr Steiner baked for the rest of the afternoon and into the evening. Mum arrived at seven with pizza and they all took a break, eating it upstairs in Mr Steiner's lounge, which was a bit higgledy-piggledy and dusty compared to their flat.

Nanny Dot produced her trumpet out of her large bag and Mr Steiner strapped on his accordion for an impromptu session of Christmas tunes. They were pretty terrible at first, making Maddie and Mum plug their fingers into their ears, but gradually they got better, ending with a rousing rendition of Rocking Around the Christmas Tree.

"Phew," panted Nanny Dot. "I'm so out of practise."

"That was amazing, Nanny," Maddie hugged her. "I can't believe you play the trumpet."

"I'm not sure I do," Nanny said. "We've agreed to play with Phil Turner's Oompah band tomorrow afternoon. We're going to need more practise." She looked at Mr Steiner, who nodded.

"C'mon," Mum said, rising. "Let's leave them to it." She reached for Maddie's hand.

"Aw, I want to hear them play."

"You'll get another chance, I'm sure. But I think you're tired and over-excited. Besides, I'd like a bit of time with my best girl before you go to bed."

"Okay," Maddie puffed out her cheeks. "I suppose so." She let Mum pull her off the sofa. "See you tomorrow, Mr Steiner."

"*Auf wiedersehen*, Maddie," Mr Steiner said. "Sleep tight."

At this Maddie turned back to him, expression anxious. "Last night?"

Mr Steiner understood immediately. "Nothing. All clear."

"And tonight?" Maddie felt her fear of the Krampus return.

"It will be fine," Mr Steiner said. "I'll keep watch."

Maddie let out her breath.

As they went out Mum asked. "What will Mr Steiner be on watch for?"

Maddie thought quickly. "Snow," she lied. "I don't want more snow."

"Oh," Mum said. She squeezed Maddie's hand. Mum didn't always understand the things Maddie was scared of. She thought some of them were daft and a product of an over-active imagination. But she did understand about Maddie's fear of snow.

Snow had taken Maddie's dad. It had taken her husband.

#

"Finally!" Nanny Dot said, as they heard the door close behind Maddie and Mum. She reached into her bag and pulled out the knitted Viking helmet. "I know who this might belong to."

"Really?" Mr Steiner leaned forward.

"I took it to 'Stop 'n' Stitch, the new wool shop on Church Street. I'd heard that the girl who owns it knits quirky hats. Her name's Meredith. She recognised this hat as soon as she saw it. She sold it at a fundraising craft fair for the homeless shelter in Great Alderton last October. She said the man who bought it worked at the shelter. She remembered because he was handsome but had a scar running down his face into his beard."

"Did Vince have a scar?" Mr Steiner asked.

"No, but he was a handsome lad."

"He works at the shelter?"

"Yes," Nanny burst out. "Can you believe it? That's where we're playing tomorrow!"

"It is meant to be," Mr Steiner said, squeezing a joyful chord out of his accordion. "On Christmas Eve too. Should we tell Lily *und* Maddie?"

"No," Nanny Dot said sharply. "He might not be Vince at all. And what if he is? What if he did just abandon them? That would hurt even more. Or worse, he might be a stalker. No, we'll go and find out what's what first."

Mr Steiner nodded. "*Und* he might not even be there."

"That's right," Nanny Dot agreed. "We won't tell them anything until we know for sure. I'm not going to ruin Christmas for them."

"*Ja,*" Mr Steiner said. "But imagine if we can make it the best Christmas ever."

He played a little jig on his accordion. Laughing, Nanny Dot tooted her trumpet.

"We should keep watch tonight," Mr Steiner said, ending his jig. "In case he comes back."

"We'll take shifts," Nanny Dot suggested. "I'll do mine first and ring you to wake you up."

"*Gut* idea," Mr Steiner said. "You are a most clever woman, Dorothy."

"I am," Nanny Dot agreed. "It's where Maddie gets it from."

10

Harry Henderson ran St Anthony's homeless hostel in Great Alderton, a large town not so very far from Wistwell. He was a slim man with a smile made crooked by a scar that ran from one corner of his mouth down his bearded chin, and a slight limp in his left leg. Both the scar and the limp were a result of an accident ten years ago, when, apparently, he'd been struck by a car. Harry always thought of it as 'apparently' because he had no memory of it. In fact he had no memory of anything before his accident at all. A severe blow to the head had left him with a brain condition called retrograde amnesia.

One day he'd woken up in a hospital bed, far, far away from Great Alderton – a busy London hospital –

and a nurse had smiled down at him and said 'Welcome back, sleepy head.'

He had no idea why he was in hospital until he tried to get up and found he couldn't. His right leg was plastered, his head shaved and bandaged, his face lacerated and bruised. Worse was the pain all over his body and the throbbing of his damaged brain.

As the days went on and he began to heal, he discovered that he'd been in a coma for five days over Christmas; that he'd been dumped by the doors to the A&E; that nobody knew who'd brought him in but it was clear from his injuries that he'd been hit by a car. He had no wallet or identification on him. No phone. Nothing, except a fiver in his jeans pocket.

He arrived during the worst blizzard since 1948, amid a bad outbreak of influenza, so that staff, already operating on a Christmas rota, found themselves overwhelmed by patient numbers.

Perhaps this is why no one had time to check the reports for missing persons or maybe it was because the police across the nation were also too busy with traffic accidents caused by the snow to issue the report for one Vincent Larkin. Whatever the reason Vincent slipped through the security net supposed to catch unlucky people like him.

His favourite nurse, Maria, gave him his name on New Year's Day because they had to call him something and as the hospital was named the Royal Harrington, but everyone called it The Harry, that's the name Maria chose.

Harry.

Harry himself selected the surname Henderson after catching an old film playing on the TV in the patients' lounge called Harry and the Hendersons.

So, when he was well enough, and with the hospital desperate to free his bed, Harry went out into the world.

The hospital had arranged for Harry to live temporarily in a halfway house for people who'd become homeless. The doctors said it was probably only a matter of time before he'd regain his memory.

But it never came back, leaving poor Harry as blank as a newborn baby. He had no national insurance number and no permanent address. Without these it was impossible to find a job that wasn't temporary and so badly paid he could never save enough to afford rent. More importantly without his national insurance number he couldn't claim housing benefit so he lost his place in the halfway house and became homeless, sleeping rough in doorways, and using cardboard for blankets. At first he used libraries to keep warm in the day and to search the internet for any trace of who he might be. But without success. He tried to find work but without access to showers and clothes he smelled bad and looked dirty.

He began to beg for food and money. When he got money he'd spend it on cheap alcohol. Getting drunk took the edge off the cold and pain.

Always, at the core of him, Harry felt that he'd lost something priceless. He just couldn't remember what it was.

Harry was lucky. A year after his accident, during a bitter December night, he realised that if he slept outside tonight he could very well die. Even in his drunken state he understood he didn't want to die, so he stumbled along to an emergency night-shelter.

There he met another homeless man, Derek, who told him about a new hostel said to be opening on King

Street run by a woman called Candy Curtis; she was looking for volunteers.

Whatever made Harry, homeless himself, think he could volunteer to help other homeless people at the new shelter was anyone's guess.

But he went the very next day, careful to turn up sober. He had a proposal for Candy. If she would offer him six months accommodation at the shelter, showers, free meals and clean clothes, he would work his socks off for her.

Candy squinted at him. She was a big woman, dressed in a multi-coloured jumper. Her hair was dyed a shocking electric blue. She crossed her arms, looked him up and down, and grunted. "Hmm," she said. "I can run this place on unpaid volunteers without making a bargain like that. You're homeless so you can have a bed anyway."

"I don't just want a bed," Harry said. "I want a purpose."

Candy stared at him some more. "No alcohol," she said. "and you go and get that shower straight away. I'll rustle up some clothes and then we'll see."

So the bargain was made.

In the end Harry stayed two years and rose to the position of deputy manager of the shelter, earning a small wage and a lot of satisfaction.

He liked working with the homeless and never forgot his own days living rough.

But Harry could never shake the nagging feeling that he'd lost something important. It gnawed at him.

He began to look for jobs working with the homeless outside of London. Although Candy was sad to lose him, she knew it was right for him to move on and gave him glowing references. He ran a shelter in Watford for two years, until the urge to move took him again. It was a pattern. He ran a hostel for two years before moving on to the next, always moving in the same northwestward direction.

He'd arrived in Great Alderton six months ago, taking the reins of St Anthony's homeless hostel. Behind him he left homeless hostels with high success rates in turning lives around. He was fast becoming known for his good work.

What drove him was an aching need to find home. Although he had no idea where that was, he let his intuition lead him. When he reached Great Alderton he sensed that this was almost it. Not quite. But almost.

Then the snow came.

It called to him. The first night it fell he finished his shift at the hostel and then went for a drive through the swirling flakes. He took random turns, letting the snow take him where it would.

It was silly and dangerous, he knew, to drive through the dark icy countryside in this weather.

The snow led him to a small town called Wistwell. The moment he drove past the sign the soft hair on the nape of his neck rose. He parked, pulling on his silly Viking hat – a buy he couldn't resist in October because it made him laugh. More importantly it made the people at the hostel laugh too – and got out of the car.

His skin prickled.

Through the snow he could just make out the names of the shops opposite. One read: Steiner's German Bakery. Next to it was a post office and next to that was a florist's: Lily of the Valley.

His throat tightened. He knew that this meant something to him but what? Frustrated, he strained to find the memories. All he came up with was a blank yet his body's reaction told him this place was important.

He took a step forwards. Stopped. Looking up he saw there was a flat above the florist shop. He could knock. No lights shone which meant that the person who lived there was either out or in bed. He couldn't wake them up. What would he say? He didn't even know why he was here.

Harry left, carefully driving the miles to Great Alderton. The next night he came again. And the night after that. He came every night, late, watching from the shadows, compelled to come. Then two nights ago he'd seen a girl sneaking out of the flat from above the flower shop. She looked about ten years old. He watched her disappear down the side of the bakery, only to re-emerge minutes later carrying two bin bags. She hurried along the icy pavement, head down and determined. When she slipped on the ice, spilling her bags, he automatically stepped forward to help.

Then she saw him and her face, illuminated by the streetlight, looked terrified. Scrambling to her feet she sprinted for the flat.

Her face shocked him – familiar but not so – and he feared suddenly being discovered loitering on the street outside of her house. It wouldn't look good at all, so he ran for his car and gunned the engine.

Yet he returned the next night. That time he'd almost been caught by a man who appeared, yelling at him, from the bakery alleyway. The little girl must have mentioned the strange man lurking in the dark. What must they think?

It was only later that he realised he'd lost his Viking hat.

He didn't dare go back the following night. It was stupid, he told himself.

If only he could get his memory back he'd know why he felt compelled to go there.

Yet his memory refused to comply.

11

It was the morning of Christmas Eve.

Maddie wanted to go with Nanny Dot and Mr Steiner to Great Alderton but Nanny wouldn't let her. It wasn't fair.

"But I want to see you play," she begged Nanny.

Nanny Dot shook her head as she packed away the sofa bed in the lounge. "A homeless shelter is no place for children."

"Why?" Maddie demanded.

"Because," Nanny said firmly. "I don't know who might be there. Homeless people often have problems."

"What sort of problems?"

"Addiction to alcohol or drugs. Some have mental health problems. It's not a place to take a little girl."

"I'm not a *little* girl," Maddie objected. "Anyway, I've seen funny Drunk Bill stumbling round the park loads of times."

"Don't call him that," Nanny said. "It's Mr Bilkes to you. And it's not funny; the poor man is ill. He's an alcoholic."

Maddie changed tack. "But you and Mr Steiner will be there and the Oompah band. I'd be safe with you."

"No, Maddie," Nanny Dot said. "You're not going. Aren't you seeing Suzy or Daisy this afternoon?"

"No," Maddie said sulkily. "Suzy's busy with her aunt and Daisy goes to her grandparents for Christmas. You should know that by now, Nanny Dot."

"Don't use that tone with Nanny," Mum scolded, coming into the lounge.

"But Mum," Maddie whined. "I want to see the Oompah band this afternoon but Nanny won't let me go. It's not fair. I was friends with Mr Steiner first."

Nanny Dot barked out a laugh. "Oh, so it's about that, is it? You think I'm stealing Mr Steiner?"

"No," Maddie denied hotly. "But it's not fair you get to go without me. Till yesterday the three of us did everything together."

Nanny Dot looked at Mum for help.

"That's right," Mum said. "I've hardly seen either of you all week; you've been so busy helping Mr Steiner I've felt quite left out."

"Really?" This made Maddie feel guilty. She wrapped her arms round Mum's waist.

"A little bit," Mum said, responding with a hug. "I know Nanny's got to go this afternoon, but I was hoping you and me could do something nice together. Then this evening you, me, Nanny and Mr Steiner, if he wants to come, can have a fabulous Christmas Eve playing games and stuffing our faces."

"What'll we do this afternoon?" Maddie asked.

"I'm not sure yet," Mum said. "But I'll think of something good."

"Okay," Maddie said, mostly mollified. "Can I still help in the bakery this morning?"

"Of course," Mum said. "Right, I'll be in the shop. I'm opening early so I can close at lunchtime." She left.

"Friends?" Nanny Dot asked Maddie.

"Um," Maddie grumbled. "Suppose so. But I really wanted to come."

"Oh dear," Nanny said. "I think you need one of Mr Steiner's magic cookies. That'll cure your grumps."

Maddie brightened. "You know, Nanny, you should take some baking to the shelter for the homeless people."

Nanny gave her a squeeze. "That's a brilliant idea," she said. "We'll ask Mr Steiner to put a bag of goodies aside."

#

The bakery was abuzz. Customers, stamping their feet as they entered, wished each other Merry Christmas, faces ruddy from the cold but glowing with good cheer. A fair number were people who'd been in during the last couple of days. Either they returned to buy yet more goods – confessing they'd already eaten what they'd bought – or they were simply coming in to give cards and greetings.

The returning customers radiated festivity. None of them seemed stressed. Maddie, noting this, secretly hugged herself because she knew the source of their happiness.

Mr Steiner's baking. And what had made Mr Steiner happy? Why, she and Nanny Dot had. And Mum's shepherd pie. And Mr Turner with his Oompah band.

There was one drawback, however, to the effect Mr Steiner's baking could have on a person. George Wilkins came into the bakery with his mum, a tired, harassed looking woman clutching a list and loaded down already with bags. Maddie noted that George wasn't carrying a single one of them.

Horrid boy!

Maddie was handing out *vanillekipferl* - beautiful little vanilla biscuits shaped like crescent moons - to waiting customers. George sneered when he saw her and made a rude gesture. His eyes lit up at the sight of the biscuits. Shoving a grubby hand past the customer in front of him, he swiped two for himself, not even bothering to offer one to his mum.

"Manners, young man," an elderly gent said. "That's not the Christmas spirit."

"I'm so sorry," George's mum mumbled. "George, put them back."

George stuffed them in his mouth, grinning, causing several customers to tut. His mum looked so upset that Maddie felt sorry for her.

"Don't worry, Mrs Wilkins," she said. "I know George isn't your fault." She gave Mrs Wilkins a biscuit, shot George her best imperious look and carried on serving the other customers.

By the time Mrs Wilkins reached the counter, something odd had happened; George was smiling. In particular he was smiling at Maddie. His eyes had taken on a sort of dazed, dewy look.

Maddie was back serving behind the counter with Nanny Dot and Mr Steiner. Mrs Wilkins had just said 'A stollen and two pretzels please," when George blurted out loudly. "You're pretty. Would you be my girlfriend?"

The entire shop seemed to fall silent. One or two people giggled. An adult murmured. "Oh, bless, he's got a crush."

Maddie stared at George, mortified. He was speaking to her. Yucky George Wilkins was asking her out. In public! It would be all over school in no time.

Then George seemed to realise what he'd said and clapped his hand over his mouth, the dewy expression replaced by one of horror. He turned to flee, pushing and stumbling his way through the queue until he was out on the street. Everyone turned to watch as he raced past the window.

The customers erupted with laughter but poor Mrs Wilkins looked hopefully at Maddie and said. "He's not so bad you know. It would do him good to have a special friend like you."

This was the point that Maddie also fled, but this time to the bakery kitchen. Her cheeks blazed with shame.

George Wilkins. Ugh.

Nanny Dot followed her. She was trying hard not to laugh and failing. "Oh," she said, clutching her belly. "Oh, Maddie. I'm sorry. Poor you. But I told you he liked you. He wouldn't be so horrid to you if he didn't."

"It's not funny, Nanny," Maddie said crossly. "It's horrible. I'll get teased about it all year. Why did he do it?"

Nanny Dot wiped her eyes. "It must be the biscuits," she said. "Mr Steiner's magic made him want to tell you the truth."

Maddie groaned.

#

They shut the bakery at twelve. Nanny Dot and Mr Steiner seemed particularly excited about playing with the band. Maddie caught them twice, whispering to each other in a corner. They shut-up as soon as they saw her. She resented being left out, and still feeling glum after the George incident, refused to eat any of Mr Steiner's baking.

"It will make you feel better," Nanny Dot said.

"I don't want to do something stupid, like George." Maddie pursed her lips.

"I don't think it was stupid," Nanny Dot said. "I think it was nice."

Maddie snorted her derision.

"You two are being silly," Mr Steiner said. "My baking is not magic. It does not change people's feelings. The *gut* taste *und* the sugar makes anyone feel happier, *ja*?"

"You're wrong, Mr Steiner," Maddie said. "My robin brought me two more berries this morning. And that," she said jabbing her finger at him, "is because it ate your apple cake."

"*Ich gebe auf*," Mr Steiner said, throwing is hands up in mock defeat. "I give up."

Maddie left Mr Steiner and Nanny Dot to practise their instruments, begrudgingly wishing them a nice time.

"Cheer up," Nanny Dot said. "We'll be back before you know it and we'll have a wonderful Christmas Eve together."

Maddie caught Nanny exchanging another meaningful look with Mr Steiner and didn't like it. They obviously shared a secret.

"Whatever," she said as she ran out of the door.

"Maddie!"

She heard Nanny Dot's call but stomped out of the alleyway without looking back.

Let them feel bad, she thought to herself. Serves them right for leaving her out.

Maddie found mum cashing up. She'd given Sally her Christmas bonus so the teenager was grinning as she pulled on her coat and hat.

"Happy Christmas," she called as she went out into the cold air.

Mum smiled at Maddie. "Why so glum, chum?"

Maddie blurted out: "George Wilkins asked me out in the bakery and Nanny Dot's mean for not letting me go with her. Christmas Eve is rubbish so far."

"Oh dear," Mum said. "Tell you what, let's take my earnings to the bank, and then watch the carol singers in the square. We'll get a bit of lunch together and you can tell me about George. Then, when we get home I've got something to show you."

"What?" Maddie asked cheering up.

"You'll see," Mum said.

"It's a surprise?"

"Sort of," Mum hesitated. "But don't get excited or you might be disappointed." She looked worried.

Maddie wanted to push for details but took the cue from Mum's expression. "Okay," she said.

She wondered what sort of surprise could make Mum frown like that. She wasn't sure it was the kind of thing she wanted to have.

She found out what it was around three o'clock, and discovered for the first time in her life that a thing could feel both wonderful and painful at the same time.

The tree lights were on and the lounge was cosy as Maddie waited for Mum to bring out her surprise. Outside, the light was waning quickly as fresh snow clouds gathered in the sky. Maddie hoped Nanny Dot and Mr Steiner would get home before the snow began to fall. Word in the town square had been that a blizzard was forecast. The thought of it made Maddie shudder.

Mum returned from her bedroom carrying a small suitcase. Maddie watched her curiously.

Mum sat down beside her and took Maddie's hand. "I've been thinking about what you said the other night – that not talking about your Dad hurt you."

Maddie held her breath.

"I've wanted to believe I was protecting you," Mum said. "But the truth is that it's been too painful for me to talk about your dad. I think I've been selfish. You deserve to know who he was."

Maddie trembled. "Did you love him, Mummy?"

"I loved him very much."

Mum reached down and undid the clasps on the old suitcase. Inside were a couple of shoeboxes and an elegant white photo album with the word 'Wedding' embossed on it. Mum picked it up, tracing her finger over the writing.

"Your dad's name was Vincent," she said. "We were only teenagers when we met. He grew up in and out of foster care. He should've been all messed up in the head but he was actually the sweetest, kindest person I knew." She removed the lid from a shoebox and drew out a handmade card with a vase of flowers painted on.

It was a beautiful painting. Maddie took it reverently. "Did he do this?"

"He did," Mum said. "He was a really good artist. It was always my ambition to open a flower shop and we planned to open the backroom as a gallery for his work. We spent hours talking about it. You know I was only nineteen when Nanny Dot secured the mortgage on this place for us. People said we were too young to start a business together, never mind get married, but we did. Those first three years struggling to build the business were so happy for us. And then when we found out I was pregnant I thought Vince was going to pop with joy. You've never seen a man so excited about the prospect of having a baby. He painted your room with little yellow ducks and flowers and funny things all over it…"

"I don't remember that," Maddie said.

"No," Mum sounded sad. "A year after he'd left, when it was clear he wasn't coming back, I painted over them. I couldn't bear to look at it."

Maddie opened the card. Inside, in her father's handwriting it read: To my Lily. One day you'll be arranging flowers like these in our very own shop while I paint in my studio. Happy Birthday. Love you always, Vince xxxxxxxxxxxxxxx

"That was for my seventeenth birthday," Mum said.

They spent a very long time looking through old photos, cards, and silly little trinkets her mother had kept. Her mother had stories to tell for every one of them. Some made Maddie laugh, others gasp. She couldn't get enough. Finally she was getting to know her father. She and Mum snuggled together as Mum turned the pages of the wedding album. Her father was so handsome, and Mum so pretty in her gown, that Maddie sighed. Nanny Dot, thirteen years younger, but still in a polka dot dress, beamed out of the group photos. It was a small wedding party but a happy-looking one.

Then, slipped into the very last page, there was a photograph that made Maddie's eyes mist up.

It was of her dad holding a tiny, red-faced baby. He was wearing a grin so wide and dazzling you could turn it upside down and use it as a rainbow,

"That's you," Mum whispered. "And your Dad."

"He didn't want to leave us, Mum," Maddie said, peering at the picture. "Look at his face."

"I've stared at that picture more times than I can count," Mum said gently. "But it won't give me an answer. I think, Maddie that we might never know why your dad left like he did, or what happened to him and we just have to be grateful that we have each other and Nanny and good neighbours like Mr Steiner." She hugged Maddie tightly. "But from now on when you want to know something about your dad I'll do my best to answer. Okay?"

"Okay," Maddie said. "Can you make me a copy of this, Mum?" She meant the photo.

"Of course," Mum said. "I'll put it in a frame for you." She glanced at the darkened window and started. "Goodness," she said. "Look at the snow. It really is a blizzard. What time is it? I expected Nanny back by now."

Maddie ran to the window. Snow whirled by so fast and thick that the streetlights were hardly visible. A car trundled past very slowly. Maddie hoped to see it stop and that Nanny and Mr Steiner would climb out but it continued to crawl along the street until its red rear lights were swallowed by snow.

Maddie felt a chill run through her. This was exactly the type of blizzard that had taken her father. Would it claim Nanny Dot and Mr Steiner too? Was the Krampus out there right now waiting to grab them?

Mum was trying her phone. "I can't get a signal," she said. "Snow must've interfered with the transmitter again. I'm sure Nanny's on her way, Maddie. They're probably just driving back very slowly. Let's start getting the food ready. If they're not here soon I'll try getting the hostel on the landline."

12

Phil Turner picked them up at two just as he'd promised. He ran around to open the passenger door of his swish BMW for Nanny Dot, bowing as he did it.

Mr Steiner noted how she giggled girlishly and slid himself and his accordion case into the back seat. He tried to ignore the flirting between the two of them and concentrate on the task ahead, but they were being rather silly. How could Dorothy behave like a schoolgirl at a time like this? Today could be the most important day in Maddie's life.

He huffed louder than he meant to at one of Phil's bad jokes. Phil looked back and said: "What's that you're saying, Hans?"

"Oh. Er, looks like snow again," Mr Steiner covered. "Hope we get back before it starts."

"Me too," Phil said. "The BMW's got a rear-wheel drive. Packs up in the snow."

"Then why didn't we take my car?" Mr Steiner asked. But he knew why. Phil wanted to impress Dorothy with his posh car. Fine lot of good that would do them if they went off the road.

"Oh, don't worry," Phil said. "Snow's not forecast to start till at least six. We'll be back long before that."

They arrived at the hostel in good time, meeting up with the other 'Oompahs' in the pay and display carpark nearby.

"Right," Nanny whispered to Mr Steiner as they followed Phil into the hostel. "We mustn't get our hopes up but I'll be on the lookout for him."

As well as their instruments they also brought a large paper sack of Mr Steiner's baking. Some of it was baking they'd set aside that morning, but once the shop was shut they'd added anything unsold. The aroma rising from the bag was fragrant with the promise of scrumptious things to eat.

A woman dressed in a Rudolph jumper welcomed them and showed them where to set up in the corner of the large dining room.

"Thank you so much," she said, accepting the bag. "These will be much appreciated."

Volunteers and residents served fruit juice, teas, and coffees from a serving hatch as hostel residents started to gather and group around tables, chatting and laughing. Many had weary faces, eyes dulled by a harsh life on the street; some bore the tell-tale signs of addiction in sunken cheeks and hollow eye sockets, but for now they were warm and safe with company on Christmas Eve.

Mr Steiner and Nanny Dot scoured the faces of the volunteers but there was no sign of Vince or a man with a facial scar. The Oompah band tuned up and the tuba started the familiar 'oom pah' beat that gave the music its name as they launched into Jingle Bells.

Residents and volunteers sang or clapped along to each cheery tune, waving tinsel and pulling crackers.

Mr Steiner lost himself in the music as he concentrated on his accordion and the pleasure of playing with the band. *Mein gott*, he had missed this.

They took a fifteen minutes break to draw breath. The jumper woman, and another volunteer, came out bearing plates of Mr Steiner's cookies which they placed on the tables. People dug in, or went outside for cigarettes or mingled. Some of the residents came to talk to the band.

There was a chorus of greetings as a slim bearded man entered the room, bundled up, hair glistening with snowflakes.

"It's started coming down early," he grinned at the jumper woman. "Going to be a busy night."

"You've missed the first half," the woman said, offering him a cookie.

As the man reached to take one, Mr Steiner spotted the scar running down his left cheek. Heart stopping, he turned to Nanny Dot, only to find her rooted to the spot, staring at the man.

"It's him," she breathed. "That's Vince."

Suddenly she was on the move, striding up to the bearded man.

"Vince," she said, planting herself firmly in front of him.

The man, cookie halfway to his mouth, blinked at her.

"Excuse me?"

"I know it's you," Nanny Dot said. "Vincent Larkin. Where in the hell have you been?" She poked her finger in his chest.

He stared at her. "You're new at the hostel, aren't you?" he said, his face softening. Clearly he thought she was a homeless person with mental health issues.

"She's with the Oompah band," jumper woman said to him. Smiling at Nanny Dot, she explained. "You must be mistaking Harry for someone else."

Mr Steiner came to stand by Nanny Dot. He peered closely at Harry. "Is this yours?" he asked, producing the knitted Viking hat.

Harry stared at the hat. He flushed guiltily. "That was you?" he asked Mr Steiner. "I'm sorry, I didn't mean any harm; I was just…"

He trailed off.

"You were spying on Lily and Maddie." Nanny Dot sounded furious. "How long for?"

"I wasn't spying," Harry denied. "I don't know who they are. Who you are. Who *are* you?"

Nanny Dot snorted. "You know bloomin' well who I am, Vince. What are you playing at?"

Mr Steiner touched her arm. "Dorothy, please." Turning back to Harry he asked: "If you really don't know Lily *und* Maddie, why were you watching their flat?"

Harry blushed a deeper crimson, making his scar stand out white "I can't explain it," he said. "I was drawn there. The place pulled me to it. It sounds ridiculous, I know. You see ten years ago I was hit by a car – that's what the doctors told me – and I have no memory before that. Ever since I got back on my feet I've been drifting …" He stopped abruptly, staring at Nanny Dot. "Who *are* you?" he asked again.

Nanny Dot had turned as white as his scar. "I'm your mother in law," she said.

The colour drained out of Harry. "You know who I am?" he whispered. "Who I was?"

Nanny Dot grabbed his hands in hers. "You are Vincent Larkin," she said.

"Why can't I remember?" Harry moaned. "I see you but I don't know you." He seemed about to faint. There were alarmed murmurings around the room.

Jumper woman sprung into practical action, placing a chair behind Vincent and pushing him down into it.

"Steady, now" she said. "Have a bite of your cookie, Harry. The sugar will perk you up."

Harry looked comically surprised to see the cookie still in his hand. Obediently he took a bite. Chewed. Took another bite. And another.

Slowly, his skin took on a normal shade. His eyes began to shine. "This taste," he whispered. "This taste. I know it. I remember it… almost. Almost." He shut his eyes concentrating. "It's so close …There was a woman, nice. She always gave me an extra two cookies, one for me, she said, and one for my sweetheart." Clenching his fists in frustration, Harry moaned. "Oh, I can't remember any more."

Mr Steiner gasped. "He is talking about my Bettina; she always gave lovers two extra cookies," he said. "Quick, get more. Get the stollen. I brought a stollen. Quick, quick…" He waved his hands at jumper woman.

Nanny Dot clutched onto Mr Steiner. Everyone was clamouring around, wanting to see what was going on.

"Give him some room," jumper woman commanded, hurrying back with a slice of Mr Steiner's stollen.

Mr Steiner grabbed it and gave it to Harry. "Eat this."

Harry eyed him doubtfully but dutifully bit into the cake. "Ugh," he almost spat it out. "Marzipan. Disgusting. I'll never know why Lily loves the stuff."

His eyes widened. "Lily!" he repeated. He devoured the whole piece of stollen, ignoring the detested taste of almonds. "Lily," he said. "I must get back. The baby..." He stopped, comprehension flooding his face. Reaching out, he grabbed Nanny Dot's hands. "Dot," he said wildly. "Dotty. You look older."

"So do you," Nanny Dot sobbed. "So do you, dear Vincent." She flung her arms around him.

Mr Steiner watched them with tears in his eyes. He had found Maddie's dad.

#

Vincent Larkin's re-awakening caused quite a stir in the hostel. Many called it a Christmas miracle and crossed themselves. Nanny Dot swore it was the magic of Mr Steiner's baking. Later on, doctors, examining the case, would conclude that as smell and taste are well-known triggers to memory the baking did help. They called it a 'powerful sensory recall'.

Whatever the reason, it was undeniable to everyone in the hostel on Christmas Eve afternoon that the transformation of Harry Henderson into Vincent Larkin was a marvel.

Over the next hour more and more of his prior life returned to him.

"The little girl I saw," Vince said to Nanny Dot. "That was Madeleine?"

"Yes," Nanny Dot nodded. She couldn't let go of his hand. "Maddie. She's ten."

"Ten," Vince shook his head. "I've missed ten years of her life. Ten whole years. What does she think? What must Lily think?" He stopped abruptly, looking pained. "Has Lily found someone else? Surely…"

"No," Nanny Dot reassured him. "No, she hasn't."

Vince let his breath out. "It must have been awful for her," he said quietly. "I can't imagine…"

"It was terrible for all of us," Nanny said. "We thought you'd abandoned Lily and the baby. Or that you'd died. But not to know what happened… That's been the worst. Still, Lily is very strong. She's brought up Maddie brilliantly."

"*Ja*," Mr Steiner agreed. "Maddie is a wonderful child."

"I want to see her," Vince said. "I want to see them both so badly. I want to go home."

"We will," Nanny Dot said. "But first let me call ahead." She finally relinquished Vince's hand and went to find a place more private to make the call.

"Do you remember what happened the night you were hit?" Mr Steiner asked Vince.

Vince frowned. "I don't remember being hit at all. We'd run out of nappies – I think the baby had the runs. I was only popping along to the Co-op so I took a fiver out of the jam jar we kept spare cash in, pulled on a coat, and went out. I should've only been ten minutes. Then…" He shrugged. "The next thing I knew I was in a hospital in London and had no idea who I was."

Mr Steiner patted his shoulder. "Poor boy. Whoever hit you must have wanted to cover it up but at least they drove you to a hospital, even if it was miles and miles away."

Vince smiled bitterly. "If they'd just left me I'd have been found. Lily would have come looking for me."

Nanny Dot returned looking flustered. "I can't get a signal, so I asked to use the hostel's landline but that's dead too."

Jumper woman bustled up. "I think the snow's taken the lines out," she said. "I hope no one's sleeping rough tonight. I'm going to set up some camp beds in here in case we need them. We're up to capacity."

Phil approached. "It's terrible out there," he said. "I can't drive in it. There's no sign of it easing off. You're welcome to stay at mine."

Mr Steiner had forgotten Phil actually lived here. He'd driven all the way over to Wistwell just so that he could have the pleasure of driving Dorothy there and back. Stupid man. *Dummkopf*!

"But we have to get home," Nanny Dot protested. "Lily and Maddie are waiting. It's Christmas Eve and we've got the best present here that they could ask for." She gestured to Vincent.

Vincent agreed. "I have to see them," he said. "I can't wait another night."

"*Ja*," Mr Steiner said. "But if it's too dangerous we should not take the risk. We must make sure you get back in one piece. I agree with Phil. The BMW will not cope in this snow. No ordinary car will."

"We need a four wheel drive," Vince said. "Who's got one?"

The question went round the room but it wasn't the sort of gathering where people owned a car, not least a four-wheel drive with their hefty price tags.

As afternoon became evening the hostel workers began to cook the evening meal.

"You need Santa to give you a lift in his sleigh," one of the residents called to Vince. It seemed everyone was trying to work out how to get him home.

People laughed. Vince smiled. "If only he could."

"Hey," another volunteer said. "You know who else will be out in this weather, besides Santa?"

Jumper woman leapt up to answer. "Gritting lorries," she said excitedly. "Yes! My brother in law drives one. They'll have attached the snow plough too." She whipped out her mobile but still couldn't get a signal. Turning to Vince," she said. "Wait here." She ran out of the room.

"Hope she remembers to put on her coat," someone said.

Half an hour later they heard a horn honking outside, although the snow was coming down so thick they could barely make out anything through the window. The dining room door opened and the woman came in, hair covered in snow, nose glowing like the Rudolph on her jumper.

"He says he can fit three in his cab," she panted. "Get your stuff and come on."

Outside, a huge yellow gritting lorry idled by the kerb, a massive snowplough buttressing its front. Christmas lights had been strung inside the cab. A burly man in a fluorescent council coat climbed down when he saw them. He stowed Mr Steiner's accordion behind the bench seat, along with Nanny Dot's trumpet and helped them up into the warm cab.

"Name's Fred," he said, once they were buckled in. "Lose me job if this gets out, but Sue told me what happened and it's a bleedin' miracle, that's what I say, so me and Big Bess are going to get you home, come heaven or high water … high snow, more like."

All the residents, volunteers and the Oompah band had crowded out, despite the weather, to wave them off.

"Thanks, Sue," Vincent shouted to jumper woman, cracking open the window.

"Get home safe," she called back. "And Merry Christmas!"

Big Bess roared into life and they set off for Wistwell at a crawl. It would be slow going but at least they were on the move.

13

Maddie stared anxiously out of the window. Not that she could see anything beyond the madly swirling flakes.

It had gone eight and Mum still couldn't pick up a phone signal. Although the landline was still working, when she tried to connect to the hostel in Great Alderton all she got was a recorded message to say that there was a fault on the line. Desperate, she checked the email to see if Nanny Dot had sent a message that way, but there was nothing.

They should have been back hours ago.

"I'm just going to see if she's at Mr Steiner's," Mum finally said. "Maybe they got back and have forgotten the time."

It was a weak hope. Maddie scrambled off the window seat. "I'll come with you."

"No need," Mum said. "You stay here and keep warm."

"No," Maddie cried. "The snow will take you too."

"I'm only going two doors down, Maddie," Mum said.

Maddie shook her head, lips set in a determined line. "And Dad was only going to the Coop. Now the snow's taken Nanny and Mr Steiner and I'm not going to let it take you as well."

Mum stared at Maddie, horrified. "Oh, sweetheart. The snow hasn't taken anyone. Nanny and Mr Steiner are probably just stuck at Great Alderton until the snow eases, that's all."

"Then why are you going to check Mr Steiner's?" Maddie demanded.

Mum seemed to deflate. "Just to make sure," she said. "And to give me something to do."

Maddie nodded. "We'll go together," she said, fetching their coats. "And if they are there we'll give them a good telling off."

"We certainly will," Mum agreed.

The snow tried to snatch them the moment they stepped out of the door. Its icy fingers plucked and pinched as they bowed their heads and marched into the wind, struggling to keep upright in the deepening swirl.

Mr Steiner's was dark and shut up. There was no light on in the kitchen or in his flat above the bakery.

Unsurprised, yet still disappointed, Maddie and Mum turned back for home.

That's when they heard the crunch of enormous tyres and the rumble of a massive engine. Yellow flashing lights appeared like two huge eyes in the street.

The gritter had come, pushing a wall of snow before it.

It juddered to a stop in front of Mum's flower shop and a man in a fluorescent jacket jumped down and trudged around to the passenger door. He hadn't seen Mum and Maddie, keeping his head down to avoid the stinging flakes. The passenger door opened and the man reached up to help someone down.

"Nanny!" Maddie yelled, recognising those polka dot boots. Heart swelling with relief she began to run towards the gritter and slipped on the slippery surface.

Maddie went down with a thud, knocking her head on one of the posts that lined the pavement.

Her vision went dark for a few seconds. When it cleared she found she was lying on her back in the snow while a horned figure crouched over her.

Her heart clutched in terror.

"Krampus," she squeaked. It had caught up with her at last.

The Krampus leaned closer, murmuring her name and reached for her. A lamp appeared next to him, held by the man in a fluorescent jacket.

Maddie gasped. The Krampus transformed into a bearded man wearing a funny horned hat. He had a scar running down one cheek and his eyes were kind. Tears trembled in them. It was a face she knew. A face she'd gazed at for so long this afternoon it was emblazoned on her memory.

But that face had been in a photograph.

"Daddy?" she whispered.

The man nodded. He smiled and a teardrop tumbled, splashing onto Maddie's nose. "It's me, Maddie."

Maddie saw Nanny Dot and Mr Steiner standing behind him, clinging to each other. Hearing a little squeal, she scrambled up to look for Mum and saw her fall to her knees as she tried to take in the sight of her long-lost husband.

"What a Christmas Eve," Fred told his wife later. "I don't mind admitting I shed a tear or two meself, but not till I was alone in my cab. I never seen anything so blimmin' marvellous."

14

Mr Steiner was exhausted but he had one thing left to do before he went to bed.

He was going to make a *sachertorte* – a gorgeously rich chocolate cake – to share with his new friends tomorrow, on Christmas Day.

He had left the family to absorb Vince's homecoming.

"Isn't it *wunderbar*?" Nanny Dot had said to him as she walked him to the door of the flat.

"*Ja. Wunderbar*," he'd smiled, looking at Nanny Dot and thinking what a fool Phil Turner had been to let this woman get away the first time.

"Make sure you're here tomorrow," she'd said as she waved him goodbye.

It was *wunderbar*, but Mr Steiner suspected that after tonight's elation tomorrow might feel just a bit awkward, especially for Lily and Vince who had an ocean of pain to put behind them. After ten years apart they were virtually strangers.

This is where the *sachertorte* came in. Mr Steiner wasn't convinced by the 'magic' of his baking the way Maddie and Nanny Dot were, but after tonight he was willing to believe in it a little bit.

So as he mixed the cake he murmured: My darling Bettina, if you can hear me tonight help me bind this cake together with all the love and joy we enjoyed for all our years. Let me share that with my friends. Let Vince and Lily heal. Let Maddie have her family back, and let Dorothy love them all."

He set the cake to bake. It was perfect when he slid it out of the oven. Tomorrow morning, after it had cooled, he would decorate it beautifully the way his father had taught him.

Content, Mr Steiner climbed into bed. Tonight he would sleep alone, but tomorrow he had friends to look forward to; he and Dorothy would play carols together.

#

Outside the snow had stopped falling. It settled deep, glistening white over the street and rooftops.

Maddie lay next to her mum. Nanny Dot had taken her bed while Dad was tucked up in the sofa bed. Maddie had crept into the lounge three times to make sure he was still there, but finally she was falling asleep.

Presents waited under the tree. Mr Steiner would be with them tomorrow. She would feed the robin. These thoughts flitted through her sleepy mind. Her last thought before she fell into slumber was a happy one.

Tomorrow she and Dad would build a snowman.

Maddie finally wanted to play in the snow. It had brought her father home.

Made in the USA
Charleston, SC
22 November 2015